THE TOOTH FAIRY

JUNIOR NOVELIZATION

Adapted by Helena Mayer

SCHOLASTIC INC.

New York   Toronto   London   Auckland
Sydney   Mexico City   New Delhi   Hong Kong

ISBN-13: 978-0-545-16817-5

ISBN-10: 0-545-16817-1

12   11   10   9   8   7   6   5   4   3   2   1   9   10   11   12   13   14/0

Designed by Rick DeMonico

Printed in the U.S.A.

First printing, December 2009

CHAPTER 1

So you want to win a hockey game? You're going to need more than a pair of skates. For starters, you'll need speed, strength, agility — and the willingness to get body-slammed by a thuggish defenseman wielding a giant stick. You'll need split-second decision-making. You'll need lightning-fast stickwork. If you want to score, you'll need to whack that puck across the ice at a hundred miles per hour. (And if you want to win without losing all your teeth, you'll need to know how to duck.)

But if you were lucky enough to live in Lansing, Michigan, and if you were smart enough to be a Lansing Ice Wolves fan, then you wouldn't need any of that. Because the Lansing Ice Wolves only needed one thing to win:

The Tooth Fairy.

*   *   *

As the clock ticked down on the third period, the score was tied, with the Fort Wayne Roughnecks coming back in a big way. The Roughnecks battled their way along the boards, trying desperately to skate the puck out of their own zone. Up in the stands, Ice Wolves fans went from shouting-and-cheering crazy to totally-and-completely-out-of-their-minds-with-the-will-to-win crazy. They leapt to their feet and screamed: "Tooth! Tooth! *TOOTH!*"

The Wolves' coach turned to his most reliable enforcer, Derek Thompson — a.k.a. the Tooth Fairy. The coach didn't have to ask Derek if he was ready to hit the ice. Standing six foot four, weighing in at 225 pounds of pure muscle, Derek was born ready.

"Let's hit somebody!" the coach growled, and Derek launched himself into the action. He bulleted across the ice, rocketing toward the Roughnecks' nearest winger. As he skated past, a row of die-hard fans lifted their shirts to reveal bold letters painted across their chests:

GOT TEETH?

Banners bobbed in the crowd:

TOOTH OR CONSEQUENCES.

TOOTH, JUSTICE, AND THE AMERICAN WAY.

THE TOOTH SHALL SET YOU FREE!

Derek ignored it all. He heard nothing but the scrape of his skates across the ice and saw nothing but the black puck, sailing toward the Ice Wolves' goal. The goalie slashed his stick through the air, whacking the puck away. It ricocheted into the wall. Every player on the ice launched themselves toward it, but the Roughnecks winger got there first. He kicked the puck along the boards, working himself into position, eyes on the net. He lifted his stick, and — *THWACK!*

Derek threw himself into the Roughneck, who slammed the wall so hard that the Plexiglas shattered. The Roughneck flew backward — but dislodged by the impact, his lower left canine tooth soared into the crowd.

"I got the tooth!" an Ice Wolves fan shouted, knocking his friend out of the way with a sharp elbow. He raised a triumphant fist in the air. "I got the tooth!"

All action on the rink halted as the Roughneck winger shakily climbed to his feet, fingers probing the empty spot in his mouth. Derek Thompson stood in the middle of the ice, bowing and beaming.

"The Tooth Fairy has struck again!" the announcer boomed, his voice nearly drowned out by the crowd.

The referee blew his whistle and jerked his head at Derek, sending him to the penalty box. No surprise there:

Derek spent so much time in the penalty box, it was equipped with his own special chair. But who cared? He'd done exactly what the crowd needed him to do. He'd blocked the shot. He'd saved the day. Now they only wanted one more thing out of him.

"You can't handle the tooth!" Derek shouted. After all, every hero needs a catchphrase. The crowd went nuts.

Derek Thompson, a.k.a. the Tooth Fairy, had never considered himself to be much of a hero. But if it meant being worshipped by thousands of screaming fans, he was willing to play one on the ice. It was all part of the game.

And Derek played to win.

Back in the locker room, Derek showered and changed into his street clothes, waiting for his teammates to rally around and thank him for saving the day . . . again.

But the team was huddling around a new guy, shaking his hand and slapping him on the back.

"What's going on here?" Derek asked irritably, bobbing his head over the crowd. Out of habit, he massaged his right shoulder, trying to keep the muscle loose. Not that it gave him much trouble anymore. He could almost imagine that it never had — if it weren't for the nasty scar etched into his skin. No matter how much he may have wanted to forget, that scar was always there to remind him.

"Thompson, there you are!" the coach boomed, waving him over. "Come meet the future of our franchise."

"Oh. Yeah," Derek muttered, letting the coach drag him toward the new guy. "The kid from Saskatchewan."

"Kid's probably only here for a cup of coffee before the Red Wings snap him up," the coach said. "But while he's here, your only job on the ice is to take care of him. Nothing else matters."

What am I, his nanny? Derek thought in disgust, giving the new guy a once-over. The kid looked pretty sure of himself for someone barely out of high school.

"Derek Thompson, Mick Donnelly, our new center," the coach said. "Mick Donnelly, Derek Thompson. Your bodyguard."

Mick flashed a cocky grin and gave Derek's hand a firm shake. Derek recognized that look in his eye, the one that said he could take on anyone or anything, anytime. Back in the old days, Derek had seen that look every time he passed a mirror.

"Hey, kid. Welcome to pro hockey," he said, thinking it might not be so bad to have someone like Mick around. Derek could show him the ropes. Maybe they'd turn out to be two of a kind, peas in a pod, brothers on the ice.

"Hey, is there an old timers' game today?" Mick said, smirking. "Didn't realize you were still playing, Grandpa. I used to be a big fan of yours."

Or maybe not.

That kid doesn't know what he's talking about, Derek fumed as he stormed out of the locker room. If he was past his prime, then why were all those fans lined up, desperate for a glimpse of him? If he was a *grandpa*, then why were half the players in the league missing teeth?

Derek waved at the fans screaming his name. He paused before a group of kids, all decked out in hockey jerseys. They gazed up at him in awe.

"Mr. Thompson, can I have your autograph?" one of the kids begged, his eyes wide and his bright red hair sticking straight up. He thrust his program at Derek.

"Sure, buddy. What's your name?"

"Gabe. I'm the third-leading scorer in my hockey league. Our team won the Mighty Mites Championship."

"That's great, Gabe," Derek said, flashing his very best superhero smile. "Good for you." He scrawled his signature across the program as the kid's dad shot him a grateful grin.

Derek wondered how long it would be before the dad sold the autograph on eBay.

"One day I'm gonna play hockey in the NHL," Gabe said eagerly. "Just like you used to."

Used to, Derek thought sourly. *Thanks for the reminder.*

"You work pretty hard at hockey, do you?" he asked.

"Uh-huh." Gabe nodded, his head bouncing up and down like some kind of bobblehead doll. "I play almost every day. I'm eight."

Derek took a good, hard look at the kid. "Okay, well, here's the thing, Gabe. And you should *all* listen." His fans leaned in, eager for a touching speech on the value of dreams and determination. Some "you just gotta believe" mixed in with "go for the gold" and, for good measure, a little "if at first you don't succeed, try, try again." They expected Derek to tell them that you could have whatever you wanted, as long as you wanted it bad enough.

Fools, Derek thought.

"You're eight," he told the kid, "and you're the third-leading scorer in your *league* behind two other *eight*-year-olds."

"Well, one is *nine*," Gabe said proudly.

Derek did his best not to roll his eyes. "Gabe, somewhere in this country there's a seven-year-old who's playing with twelve-year-olds and outscoring *them*." He paused for a moment to let it sink in. "And there are a bunch like him at every *rink*."

The kid's eyes were welling up.

It hurts now, kid, Derek thought. *But not as much as it would hurt later. Trust me.*

"And when the time comes, *those* kids will fight it out and only a handful of them will get signed," he continued. Now all the kids looked like they were about to cry. "See, kids, for every player that actually makes it to the NHL, there are ten *million* kids who never had a prayer. And say you *do* make the NHL — you *won't*," he added quickly, "but say you do. . . . Before you can say 'slap shot,' you're pushed down to the minors with a blown-out shoulder and no way back —" He stopped himself, and drew in a deep breath. This wasn't about him, or his bum shoulder. This was about looking out for the kids. "How are you gonna feel then? Lower your expectations. That's how you're gonna be happy!" He handed the signed program back to the kid. "There you go, Gabe."

The kid's father yanked him away, as if afraid that Derek was contagious.

"It's for their own good!" Derek shouted, as the rest of the parents dragged their weepy kids off to the parking lot. "One day they'll thank me!"

Just not any day soon.

CHAPTER 2

Derek had bought the car with his NHL signing bonus. *Just the beginning,* he'd thought, signing the papers on a brand-new Camaro, blue as the sky. *Anything I want,* he'd thought. *Sky's the limit.*

But it had turned out that Derek's shoulder was the limit. The muscles and tendons in his shoulder had blown out with one bad hit. After that, it was back to the minors, back to a microscopic paycheck that would barely cover his rent. That blue Camaro was the first and last new car he'd ever own. It was a symbol of everything he could have had. He hated it. But it was better than taking the bus.

Derek pulled up to his girlfriend's house and headed inside without knocking. Carly and her kids were in the kitchen, chowing down on a feast of burgers and fries. Derek gave Carly a quick kiss hello, then ruffled her daughter's hair. Tess squirmed out of reach, giggling with delight. Derek wasn't big on kids, but even he had to admit that Tess was adorable. Maybe it was the six-year-old's curly brown hair or her spunky grin. Maybe it was just the way she looked at him, like he could do no wrong. Derek had dated women with kids before, but Tess was the first kid he honestly hadn't minded having around.

Her brother, Randy, was another story. A surly, stubborn, angry twelve-year-old story. Derek couldn't do anything wrong when it came to Tess, but with Randy? He couldn't do anything right.

Derek dipped a couple french fries into a puddle of ketchup, then shoved them onto his teeth like fangs. "I vant to suck your blood," he teased Tess. Ketchup dripped onto her plate. As she laughed, Derek gave her a wounded look. "Vat? Vat are you looking at? Vy aren't you afraid?"

"Because those are french fries!" Tess sputtered.

"Noooooooo!" Derek moaned. "I can't eat french fries!" He shot a glance at Randy, wondering if he'd finally made the kid crack a smile.

But Randy just stared grimly at his burger, as if Derek wasn't even there.

"French fries are fatal to vampires!" Derek moaned, grabbing his throat and pretending to choke. Tess shrieked gleefully, then stood up and shoved a fry onto her own tooth, trying to be just like Derek.

Then she screamed, "Mommy, my tooth came out!"

"Congrats!" Carly gasped, swinging her daughter off her feet.

Derek didn't get the big deal — he knocked guys' teeth out every night. He raised a fist in a halfhearted *yay*.

"The tooth fairy's going to visit me tonight!" Tess squealed.

"What?" Derek exclaimed. "*I'm* the Tooth Fairy!"

As Tess dissolved into giggles all over again, Randy rolled his eyes. "I thought you were a vampire," he said. "You've got an inconsistent mythology, man."

Carly shook her head. "Randy, do you feel like playing your guitar for Derek?" She turned to Derek, looking hopeful. "He's getting so good. Who knows? He might be the next Santana."

Randy unloaded another eye roll. "I've got a lot of homework," he mumbled. "Can I be excused?"

Carly's face fell, but she nodded.

Randy slipped out of the room. "I think he's finally warming up to me, don't you?" Derek said sarcastically.

Carly just sighed. But before she could say anything, Tess started pushing against her legs. "Mommy, it's time for you to go now, so Derek can start babysitting."

"Very soon, sweetie," she said, laughing. "Why don't you go get your jammies on?"

Once Tess was gone, Carly got serious again. "Maybe if you and Randy had some one-on-one time?"

Derek shrugged. "Sure, I can do that. As long as I don't have to be alone with him."

Carly looked like she didn't want to laugh, but she laughed anyway. She always did.

There was a honk outside. "Okay, Renee's here!" Carly said, jumping up and grabbing her purse. She gave Derek a quick kiss good-bye. "Oh, wait! The tooth fairy."

She started digging through her purse, but Derek grabbed her hand. "It's okay," he assured her. "I got it."

Just then, Tess popped back into the room. "Look, I put on my pajamas!" she announced.

"Oh, no!" Derek said, in his vampire voice. "Dracula has come back from the dead! Your french fries were not powerful enough!" He lunged for her. Screaming, she raced down the hallway, Derek hot on her heels.

Neither of them noticed when Carly slipped out the door.

Derek didn't mind babysitting. Especially the part where he got to ship the kids off to bed and play poker with his hockey buddies. Usually they played at Derek's place, but no one minded using Carly's instead.

Lucky for Derek, Carly didn't mind either.

"So, what do you guys think of Donnelly?" one of Derek's teammates, Brad, asked.

The guys all spoke at once in their eagerness to lay on the praise.

"Man, that kid's fast!"

"Next Gretzky!"

Derek scowled. "Can we just play cards?"

"It's to you," Brad pointed out.

"Oh." Derek looked down at the table, where his pile of chips had dwindled to nothing. "I'm a little short."

The guys all groaned. Derek ignored them. His luck was turning, he could feel it. He could win this hand — he just needed a way to ante up. "Check this out." Derek grabbed a scrap of paper off the kitchen table and signed his name to it. "That autograph right there will get you ten bucks on eBay. I can sign ten of these. That's like a hundred bucks."

The guys shook their heads.

"Come on," Derek pleaded. "I'm good for it."

But it was a no-go. There were no leftover bills in his wallet, no cash in any of the coat pockets, no spare change in the spare-change drawer.

"Doesn't one of the kids have a piggy bank or some-thing?" Brad teased.

"Very funny," Derek said, getting desperate. Then he

remembered: There *was* cash in the house. He tiptoed down the hall, into Tess's bedroom. *I'm just borrowing it,* Derek told himself. And then, very, very quietly, he reached under her pillow and pulled out a five-dollar bill.

"How's *that* for a comeback?" Derek crowed to the boys, flipping through his winnings as the front door opened.

"It smells like man feet in here," Carly teased, as she came into the kitchen and surveyed the damage. Empty pizza boxes were strewn across the table. The floor was scattered with grease-stained paper towels and crushed soda cans. "Although it looks better than I expected."

The guys left in a hurry — probably afraid that Carly would make them help clean up. Derek grinned. It wasn't so bad cleaning, not with Carly there to keep him company.

"*Moooooooommy!*"

Carly raced for Tess's bedroom, Derek right behind her.

"Honey, what happened?" Carly swept the sobbing six-year-old into her arms.

"My — my — tooth — is — gone!" Tess sputtered.

Carly rubbed a hand slowly against Tess's back, trying to calm her down. "That's because the tooth fairy took it," she said gently.

Tess scrunched up her face like she was about to start screaming again. "But there's no money! I looked."

"Oh." Carly wrinkled her forehead, confused. "We'll look together. I'm sure it's somewhere."

"It's not!" Tess buried her face in the pillow, kicking her legs against the mattress.

Derek felt like she'd kicked him in the stomach. "The vampire is back again!" he said, hoping to distract her. Anything to get her to stop crying before Carly figured out where that tooth fairy money had gone.

Carly glared at him. "This is *not* a vampire moment." She turned back to Tess. "Maybe they took the tooth to check it on the . . . toothmeter, to see how much it's worth before they bring you the money," Carly said haltingly. "Right, *Derek*?"

Derek sighed. What *was* it with kids and their silly fantasies? "Yeah, that's how the whole tooth thing works," he said halfheartedly.

"No!" Tess shouted. "That's not how it works! You put the tooth under your pillow, the tooth fairy flies into your room when you're sleeping, takes the tooth, and leaves a dollar!" She slumped onto the bed. Tears started leaking out again. "Where is it?"

"All right," Derek said, whipping out his roll of cash. He started unrolling the bills one by one. "Tell me to stop when the tooth fairy's been here."

Carly grabbed his wrist. "Derek." Her voice was icy.

"I'm just . . ." Derek looked back and forth between Carly and Tess. He didn't know which one confused him more. "Look, Tess, you're a big girl. You're six years old. So let's get this over with. There's no such thing as the tooth fairy —"

"*There it is!*" Carly yelled over him, palming a bill from her purse and pretending to draw it from under the bed.

Tess examined it in wonder. "How did it get down there?"

"Well, you probably rolled over and moved your pillow, and the window's open," Carly explained quickly, "so it probably blew off."

Tess bought it. Soon she was calm enough to go back to bed — her fist curled tightly around the five-dollar bill. As soon as Tess was asleep, Carly shoved Derek into the living room, still enraged. "What happened?"

"I was short in the game," Derek admitted, "and the guys were ragging on me —"

"So you stole her tooth fairy money?" Carly asked.

Okay, it sounded bad when she put it like that.

"Borrowed!" Derek protested. "I was gonna give it back. I forgot. People forget."

Carly shook her head. "So then your bright idea was to handle it by telling Tess there's no tooth fairy."

What's the big deal? Derek thought. "Carly, come on," Derek said. "Of all the crazy things people tell their kids, the idea that a little fairy is going to fly through the window and buy their teeth has to be one of the dumbest —"

"The tooth fairy is a wonderful childhood fantasy!" Carly snapped. "It teaches kids to use their imaginations, to dream a little. To say 'What if'!"

Derek jumped in. "See, there's a reason so many people are unhappy. Because they're clinging to some version of 'What if'."

Carly was standing very stiff, very straight, and very far away. "So if something's a little difficult, don't bother?"

"Basically," Derek said. Now she was getting it.

"That's ridiculous!" she shouted. "Then how does anyone ever become president? Or win an Olympic gold medal? Or just get an 'A' in algebra?"

This was like quicksand. The more Derek talked, the deeper he sunk. "You're saying that believing in the tooth fairy will help Tess grow up to be president?"

Carly turned her back on him, like she couldn't even be bothered to respond. "I'm going to bed. And *you're* leaving."

She shoved him out the door and slammed it behind him.

CHAPTER 3

Derek couldn't sleep.

It wasn't because of the lumpy mattress or the leaky sink or the weird buzzing noise his refrigerator had started making.

And it definitely wasn't because Carly was mad at him. That's what he told himself, anyway. If she wanted to go nuts about some silly fairy, that was her problem. Not his.

No, it was the annoying itch on his back, right between his shoulder blades. He kept trying to scratch it, but couldn't quite reach without ripping his shoulder out of his socket. He grunted in frustration and turned over onto his stomach, squeezing his eyes shut. All he had to do was ignore the itch, and eventually it would go away.

Ignore. The. Itch.

But it was no use. He felt like his skin was crawling off

his body. Or like something was crawling around *beneath* his skin . . .

Derek shuddered, and grabbed his pillow. Forget it — he'd hit the couch and fall asleep in front of the TV.

But there was something underneath his pillow. It was a piece of paper, the size of a parking ticket. Nothing weird about that.

Except that it was glowing.

Derek turned on the light. He sat up in bed. Drew in a deep breath. And read the strange note.

VIOLATION 701369 it said at the top, in ominous black type. **TOOTH FAIRY DIVISION DEPARTMENT OF DISSEMINATION OF DISBELIEF. You are hereby summoned to appear . . .**

"What the —" Derek broke off reading as the itch on his back intensified. This wasn't any ordinary itch. It felt like his skin was on fire. He jumped out of bed and rushed to the mirror.

That was a mistake.

"Whaaaaaaaaaa —?" Derek stared into the mirror, slack-jawed, all the air whooshing out of him like he'd taken a puck to the gut. He stood frozen as two giant, billowing wings sprouted out of his back. His sleep shirt began to transform itself into something . . . else. Something shimmering and pink and leotard-like. The mirror only showed him from the waist up. Derek gulped and looked down at himself. A frilly pink tutu circled his waist. And on his feet? Sparkling pink slippers.

This is a nightmare, Derek told himself. *So WAKE UP!*

But he didn't wake up. Not before a shimmering whirlwind erupted into the room. The pink tornado headed straight for him. Instinctively, Derek's hands closed over an imaginary hockey stick and he got into a fighting stance.

The cyclone sucked him into a swirling vortex of pink. A moment later, the whirlwind winked out of existence. The room was empty . . . except for Derek's lingering scream.

Derek stopped screaming and opened his eyes. He found himself in a grand concourse. Carved marble columns and windows stretched to unimaginable heights. Stars twinkled in the curved ceiling, brighter and more magnificent than the night sky. But that wasn't the strangest thing.

The strangest thing was that the concourse was filled with people, people with only one thing in common: They were all dressed as fairies. Many had wings.

With a gasp, Derek reached behind him. His hand closed over something soft and feathery. His *wings*.

Above him, giant screens flickered with information, like a train station's arrival and departure boards. But these boards made no sense. Strange names and addresses scrolled down, each notated with alerts like CHILD ASLEEP, TOOTH UNDER PILLOW, and ASSIGNMENT COMPLETE.

Trying not to meet anyone's eye, Derek inched his way toward what looked like an information booth.

"Thompson?" A voice called out before he got up the nerve to speak. "Derek Thompson?"

Derek craned his neck toward the majestic ceiling. "Yes!" he shouted. "Yes! I'm here! Is it God? I'm here, God!"

Fingers snapped in front of Derek's face, and he looked down again. "*You're* God?" he asked the little man standing before him. "How disappointing."

With his pinched face, thick glasses, and pocket protector tucked into an ill-fitting fairy uniform, the guy looked more like a high school debate captain.

"I'm Tracy, your caseworker," the man said, eyes fixed on his BlackBerry. "Walk with me." He didn't bother to check that Derek would follow. Instead, typing away on his Black-Berry, he strode through the terminal. Derek hurried after him, nearly crashing into two fairies in long, swirling robes.

"Fairy Krishnas," Tracy explained, realizing that Derek had stopped. Then his eyes widened as he took in tutu-clad Derek for the first time. "What are you *wearing*?"

"What are *you* wearing?" Derek shot back defensively. Okay, so he was the only guy in the place in a tutu, but *everyone* was in some kind of bizarre Halloween gear, including Tracy. "Where *am* I?"

A crowd had begun to form around them, as the fairies realized that a stranger — a strangely dressed stranger — was in their midst.

"Who is this guy?" one of them asked his friend. Neither of them were stuck with tutus *or* pink slippers, Derek noticed irritably. They got pants.

"Human," another of the fairy men guessed. "D-O-D."

They were the magic words, whatever they meant. The fairy gawkers scattered, shooting Derek dirty looks.

"Dream killer," Tracy explained to Derek. He shook his head in disgust. "You should all be locked up where you can't hurt anyone."

"What did I do?" Derek asked, more confused by the second. "Why am I here?"

"You're a D-O-D."

It didn't make any more sense the second time. "What?"

Tracy sighed. "A Disseminator of Disbelief. And for the record? I don't like your kind. I don't like the way you look all confused like you don't know why you're here." He lowered his voice to mimic Derek's befuddled growl. *"What did I do? Why am I here? Why do I suddenly have wings?"*

"Whoa, man, settle down!" Derek urged him. "What'd I do to you?"

Tracy stiffened. "I don't like the casual way you say 'Settle down. What'd I do to you?'"

"Tracy . . . isn't that a girl's name?" Derek smirked.

Tracy pressed his lips together. His face went very red, then very white. He closed his eyes and swallowed hard. Then he opened his eyes and plastered a tight, businesslike smile on his face. "I'm going to ignore that. We'll get your uniform sorted out later. Now, let's get you through registration and training."

"Training for *what*?!" Derek shouted.

"Oh." Tracy cleared his throat. "You, Mr. Thompson, are going to serve time as a tooth fairy."

"Oh," Derek replied in a polite, isn't-that-nice, tea-party kind of voice.

Then he ran.

"Stop him!" Tracy shouted as Derek raced through the terminal, barreling through a pack of fairies like they were Roughnecks with wings. Footsteps pounded behind him. He darted around a gang of fairies with briefcases and BlackBerries, skidded past a gaggle of old lady fairies knitting sparkling tutus, leapt over a kid-sized fairy on a flying skateboard — and plowed straight into a giant fairy dressed like a professional wrestler. Derek bounced off his chest and slammed backward, toppling to the floor. Two pint-sized fairies swooped in to grab his ankles. Two more grabbed his wrists. They dragged him across the terminal, dumping him in a bruised pile at Tracy's feet.

"Ow!" Derek grunted as his head smacked the floor.

Grudgingly, Tracy gave him a hand and yanked him to his feet. "Now, where were we?"

Right about here, Derek thought. "Somebody wake me up!" he screamed. "Please! I'm having a nightmare! Help me!"

Tracy poked him in the chest. Hard. "The nightmare's just beginning, buddy."

Derek glared down at the puny little man, who dared to poke *Derek Thompson*, star of the Lansing Ice Wolves. "What're you doing?" he growled, giving Tracy a hard poke back.

"You want to go?" Tracy snapped, grabbing Derek's ear. "'Cause I'll go."

"What?" Derek tugged Tracy's ear, too, tempted to yank the man off his feet. "No, I don't want to go! I just want to know why I'm dressed like Tinker Bell."

Tracy wriggled out of Derek's grasp. "I know Tinker Bell," he said gruffly. "Tinker Bell is a friend of mine. And you, sir, are no Tinker Bell." He whipped out a long, sparkling wand, brandishing it at Derek like a weapon.

"Whattya going to do," Derek scoffed, "pull a rabbit out of a hat?"

"Fairy fight!" someone shouted, and a circle of fairies formed around them. A wand went flying toward Derek. He snatched it out of the air. It looked like a piece of junk, but he gave it an experimental shake — and a puff of fairy dust popped out of one end, right into his eyes.

"Wait!" he shouted, waving blindly. "I can't see!"

Something poked him in the chest, then the shoulder, then the face. Tracy's wand. Still blinded by the fairy dust, Derek reached out. His hand closed around the wand, and he snapped it in two. A hush fell over the crowd.

A crisp voice cut through the silence. "*What* is going on out there?"

Derek's vision slowly cleared. A thin, tall, stern-looking woman stood before them, her lips pursed in disapproval. Two magnificent wings arched from her back. She tilted her head, looking back and forth between Derek and Tracy, clearly waiting for some kind of explanation.

"He broke my wand!" Tracy whined.

"It's his fault!" Derek said at the same time.

"Stop it!" the woman snapped in a crisp British accent. She spoke quietly, almost gently, but something in her voice was still sharp. "You're behaving like leprechauns."

"Sorry, Lily," Tracy said, "but he's got an attitude."

Lily, whoever she was, gave him a thin smile. "Oh, I'm well aware of his attitude, believe me. Hello, Mr. Thompson."

Derek flinched. How did she know his name?

"Sorry about the foul-up with your outfit," she said. "Budget problems. We should have you properly outfitted for your first call."

"Oh, great," Derek said sarcastically. He decided it was probably best to go along with these crazy people until he found an escape route . . . or until he woke up.

Lily held out her hand. Tracy scurried toward her, depositing the clipboard in her open palm. She stamped something across the top page. "You, sir, are guilty of disseminating disbelief," she told Derek. "Killing dreams. Committing first-degree murder of fantasy —"

"Wait," Derek said. "Is this because of what happened with Tess?"

Lily raised an eyebrow. "Do I look like I'm done talking? Am I done talking? *Am* —"

Derek hadn't felt like this since his days of getting sent to the principal's office. "I don't know."

"You just interrupted me *again* while I was admonishing you for interrupting me," Lily said incredulously. "Do I not look official enough? Shouldn't you be more in awe of someone with wings than someone without? I could fly up and do something crazy. Maybe I breathe fire. You don't know."

"I'm sorry," Derek said again, glancing around for somewhere to take cover in case flames suddenly flared from her mouth. "I didn't mean to interrupt."

Lily gave him a smile. "That's better. In order to pay your debt to humanity, you are hereby ordered to serve time as a tooth fairy. The typical sentence is one week. However, because you have the nerve to actually *call* yourself the Tooth Fairy and thus make a mockery of everything we stand for, I'm sentencing you to two weeks —"

"Hey, man, that's not fair!"

"Shhhh!" Lily wagged a finger in his face. "Interrupting. Remember, from one second ago?"

Lips firmly shut, Derek nodded.

"I'll tell you what's not fair. You're out there killing the dreams of innocent children."

She paused, and Derek wondered whether he was supposed to say something — but he didn't want to risk interrupting her again.

And he had no idea what to say.

Lily sighed impatiently, then nodded at Tracy and flicked a hand in dismissal. "Take him through training."

It'll all be over soon, Derek promised himself, as Tracy led him away. *Sooner or later, I'll have to wake up.*

He just hoped it was sooner.

CHAPTER 4

The nightmare continued. Tracy dragged Derek down a series of increasingly narrow corridors and shoved him into a decrepit old classroom.

Derek didn't have any fight left in him. He squeezed himself into a tiny chair meant for someone half his size as Tracy set up a rusted old film projector. Then Tracy shut off the lights. A blurry, faded image lit up the pull-down screen at the front of the room.

FANTASY FILMS PRODUCTIONS PRESENTS . . .

AN INCONVENIENT TOOTH

The words faded from the screen, replaced by a scruffy little kid biting into an apple. His eyes went wide, and he gasped. Loudly.

Kid's not the best actor, Derek thought sourly.

"Look, Mother!" the kid said, enunciating clearly. "My tooth came out!"

His mother swept onto the screen, complete with fifties beehive and lacy apron. "That's *wonderful*, Jimmy." She was even worse than the child. "You put that tooth under your pillow tonight and the tooth fairy will bring you a dime."

"Well, isn't that swell, Mother!" the boy said heartily. He swung a fist through the air.

Derek snickered.

Back on the screen, time sped forward to the next morning. Little Jimmy was tucked cozily into bed. He stretched in an exaggerated waking-up gesture, then reached under his pillow and pulled out a bright, shiny dime.

"Oh, what a happy day for little Jimmy," a voice-over announced. "And who made this happy day possible?" The camera panned across an army of tooth fairies, their wings spread wide and their smiles bright.

Derek groaned and planted his face on the desk.

At least they gave Derek something new to wear. Not that it was much of an improvement.

But at least it wasn't a tutu.

And it wasn't *pink*.

Once he was suitably outfitted, Tracy deposited him at a

dingy supply room. "Get your supplies from Jerry," he said. "Then we're off to flight school."

"I can hardly wait," Derek said dryly.

The supply room was lined with shelves, all of them overstuffed with cardboard boxes, jars, tubes, files — *junk*. A hunched little man with tattered wings was perched on a ladder, pawing through a sagging cardboard box.

As Derek entered the room, Jerry's eyes lit up. A mischievous grin danced across his face. "Oh, look who it is! Mr. Dream Popper. So, it made you feel good to lie to the kid?"

"No, it didn't." Besides, Derek hadn't lied. It was just brutal honesty, whether they liked it or not.

"Now look, if you're gonna be a fairy, you gotta be ready." The little man drew Derek in close and tipped his head toward Derek's ear. "Although . . . there is a pill," he whispered. "You take it, you don't have to do this."

"Really?"

"No. Just kidding."

The words were like a slap across the face.

"See, you *believed* for a second," Jerry crowed. "And then I took it away. Be mad at me, I don't care. Let's get to work."

Jerry paused at a long countertop and dug something out of a bulky gray bin. "Pay attention. First, your tool pouch." He handed a thick leather pouch to Derek, who examined it without much interest. "Waterproof, plenty of compartments." Jerry rummaged through a couple of messy drawers before pulling out a long, spindly metal rod. "Wand. It's a tooth detector, radar jammer." He pointed to a bright red button near the bottom. "All-Purpose Magic Generator Button. Does whatever you want. But you have to believe or it doesn't work, so it's pretty useless to humans."

Great, Derek thought, taking the useless wand.

"And don't lose this," Jerry added, pulling something small and pluglike out of another drawer.

"What is it?"

"iPod adapter."

"What's that for?" Derek asked.

Jerry rolled his eyes. "Listening to your iPod. You get a free iPod, you know?"

"Really?" Derek asked. Finally, some good news!

Jerry smirked. "No, just kidding."

Jerry piled supplies in Derek's arms. "This is your invisibility spray. When you use it, only other fairies will be able to see you. Shrinking paste. Squeeze some into your mouth, and it shrinks you down to about six inches. I would recommend a test run. Do you want to?" He grinned eagerly. "I'll do it with you. We'll jump into each other's hands."

Derek shifted away. "No, I'm good."

"You sure?" Jerry came closer and waved the shrinking paste in his face. "I think you're curious."

Don't make eye contact with the crazy, Derek thought, *and maybe it'll get bored and leave.* "Can we move on?"

"Want a mint?" Jerry said excitedly, switching gears like a hyperactive five-year-old.

"Uh, sure." Derek took the dusty, oblong mint out of Jerry's hand and popped it into his mouth, wrinkling his nose at the peculiarly bitter taste. "This is really — *ARF. ARF? WOOF! WOOF! ARF!*"

"Dog bark mints," Jerry said, eyes twinkling. "They come in handy."

Derek spit the mint halfway across the room. He pressed his fingers to his lips, wondering if the effect was permanent. Only one way to find out. "For what?"

At least he wouldn't bark like a dog for the rest of his life. That was something.

Not much, but something.

"Cats, mailmen, other dogs," Jerry explained. "Or in case a child that you scared comes after you."

This was getting ridiculous. "How many times do I have to say I'm sorry?"

"Six times."

That easy? Why hadn't anyone just *told* him? "I'm sorry," Derek said quickly. "I'm sorry, I'm —"

"I'm just kidding." Jerry waved a hand in disgust. "You're a little dull up there," he scoffed, pointing at Derek's head.

Then he started sorting through drawers again, tossing more "helpful" supplies on the pile. "Here's knock-out gum." Jerry pulled object after object out of his cluttered drawers, flinging them away once he'd decided they weren't right. "Giggly gas. Cat-Away," he muttered, tossing them aside one by one. "Bird-Be-Gone." He waved the tube in Derek's face. "Stealth Slippers. Make you all nice and stealthy. Also, very fashionable. Travel Tutu. When you need a tutu on the go-go."

Derek took a closer look at the box containing the Travel Tutu. It didn't look big enough to hold a tube of travel toothpaste. He looked closer — and the box exploded in his face, a full-sized tutu bursting out of nowhere, tangling him in a net of shimmering pink tulle.

"Snore blocker," Jerry continued, ignoring the chaos. "Oh — this can be useful." He held out a delicate silver flute. "The sleep flute."

No way. It was bad enough they'd forced Derek into the fairy costume. "I'm not taking the sleep flute."

"You're gonna want the sleep flute," Jerry wheedled, sounding like a mother trying to convince her child to swallow some foul-tasting medicine.

"I don't *want* the sleep flute."

"They never want the sleep flute," Jerry grumbled. He threw it on the pile with the rest of the discards. A moment later, he snatched a small pouch from the nearly empty drawer. "Ah! This is what I was looking for. In case you get caught . . . amnesia dust. Throw a pinch, and the kid forgets everything that happened for the last few seconds."

What kind of fool does he think I am? Derek thought, rolling his eyes. "Yeah, right."

Jerry opened the pouch, dipped his fingers in, and flung a pinch of dust in Derek's face. "That's how it works."

"That's how what works?" Derek asked, confused.

Jerry smiled, glancing around like he wished there was someone else to enjoy the joke. "You throw a pinch, the kid forgets everything that happened in the last few seconds."

What kind of fool does he think I am? Derek thought, rolling his eyes. "Yeah, right."

Jerry tossed another handful of dust in Derek's face. "That's how it works," he said.

"How what works?"

Jerry cackled, and did a shuffling little dance of glee. "Amnesia dust. You throw a pinch, the kid forgets everything that happened the last few seconds." Without waiting for a response, he blew a puff of dust into Derek's face. "That's how it works."

"How what works?"

Jerry just shook his head. "Never gets old." But before he could play again, his cell phone rang. Jerry flipped it open and pressed it to his ear. "Uh-huh." He hung it up and beamed at Derek. "That was my supervisor. They made a mistake in your paperwork. You're free. Don't have to do this."

Derek felt like the Ice Wolves had just won the Stanley Cup. *"Really?"*

"Just kidding," Jerry said perkily. "I'm just trying to see how much I can get away with."

Derek resisted the urge to strangle the man. Barely.

"Okay, you came in here a disbelieving hockey player — you're going out there a fairy," Jerry said proudly, giving him a hearty slap on the back. "Good luck to you!"

Maybe that's it, Derek thought hopefully. *Maybe I can finally go home.*

But Tracy was waiting for him outside the storage room, and the anxious fairy didn't lead him back to the real world. Instead, he took Derek to an imposing white door. The sign across the top made Derek's stomach lurch.

FAIRY FLIGHT TRAINING CENTER

He would never have admitted it to Tracy, or to anyone, but Derek had a deep, dark secret. He was afraid of heights.

The walls were white. The floor was white. The miles-high ceilings were white. And Derek's wings were white.

The wings that they were expecting him to use to *fly*.

"They" were Tracy and a craggy old fairy named Duke, who stood at the edge of the room behind a console of buttons, dials, and levers, waiting for Derek to strut his stuff.

Derek was pretty sure he had no stuff.

They'd stuck him in the middle of the room, on top of a grate. Derek squinted down into the darkness, barely able to make out an enormous fan.

"Now, flying is tricky," Tracy warned him. "You gotta learn how to use your wings."

"I think I have a bad . . . wing," Derek said nervously. "Hockey injury."

Duke snorted. "That's one I never heard before."

"No, really," Derek insisted, getting a little desperate. "It's not the same as the other —"

A loud whoosh drowned out the rest of his words. The fan beneath Derek's feet began to whir, and a jet stream of wind shot him twenty feet into the air.

"Aaaaaaaah!" Derek screamed.

"Flap!" Tracy shouted. "Use your wings!"

Derek tried. He flapped his wings like a spastic bird. The motion sent him spinning out of control.

"I'm crankin' this baby up!" Duke shouted. "I think you're ready to practice FOA!"

"What?" Derek yelped, still tumbling helplessly. He was starting to get nauseous.

"Flying Object Avoidance!" Duke pulled out a tennis racket and a basket of tennis balls. "Watch out!" he called. "A seagull!"

A tennis ball went zinging toward Derek. It hit him square in the forehead.

"A flock of pigeons!"

Before Derek could get out of the way, a ball slammed into his chest. Another hit his shoulder, knocking him into a wild spin.

"You're flying over Wimbledon!" Duke shouted. He'd ditched the racket and brought out a tennis ball machine. The balls shot out like machine gun–fire. Derek flapped his wings as hard as he could. He tried not to wonder what would happen when Duke got bored and turned off the fan.

Because he had a bad feeling that there was only one thing more painful than flying:

Landing.

Waiting in line in Fairyville was just as boring as waiting in line in the real world. But at least while Derek was standing in line, no one was banging tennis balls at him or stuffing him with dog bark mints.

Unfortunately, like all lines, this one eventually brought him to the front.

Derek found himself standing across from an extremely bored fairy, who was sorting through piles of forms. She barely looked up at Derek.

"Raise your right hand, repeat after me," she said, in a mechanical monotone. "I, fill in your name . . ."

Derek sighed. "I, Derek Thompson . . ."

". . . swear to uphold and perform . . ."

". . . swear to uphold and perform . . ."

". . . all of the duties, responsibilities, and obligations . . ."

". . . all of the duties, responsibilities, and obligations . . ."

". . . of a tooth fairy."

Derek opened his mouth. But he couldn't bring himself to say it.

"*Of a tooth fairy*," she said again, finally meeting his eyes.

"Of a tooth fairy," Derek finally said, defeated.

"Now flap your wings and spin around."

Derek turned around and gave his shoulders a shake. The wings flapped. Or, at least, one of them flapped. The other one just hung there limply, like a broken feather. The woman handed Derek a book of coupons. "Welcome aboard," she said, turning back to her forms. "These coupons are all redeemable in the gift shop."

Pretty sure he had no use or desire for a new tutu, 25% off or not, Derek ripped the coupon book in half. "All right!" he shouted, storming away. "It's real! Tooth fairies exist!" He stomped down a series of hallways at random and found himself in front of an open office door. Lily sat inside, smiling serenely, as if she'd been waiting for him.

"Can't I just pay a fine?" Derek pleaded. "Or you could assign me to be the Big Brother of a poor fairy kid. Or I could pick up garbage along the fairy highway." He hesitated. "As I say that, I realize I'd rather pay a fine."

She gave him a sour look. "Sorry." No one in the history of apologies had ever meant one less. "You're booked. Your sentence starts tomorrow. You'll —"

"Well, then, can I put it off? Because right now I've got the coach breathing down my neck like crazy, and I'd *like* to try to patch things up with my girlfriend. . . ." He trailed off. "And . . . the interrupting thing. Sorry."

"Any assignment you miss, you get another week," Lily informed him. "And if you fail your terms of service, or tell anyone you're the tooth fairy, your time will be extended *indefinitely*." She paused. He wanted to vomit. "Good-bye, Mr. Thompson. We'll be in touch."

Before he could drop down on his knees to beg for his freedom, she flung a handful of fairy dust in his face.

He fell to the floor.

A whirlwind raged around him and sucked him into a bottomless vortex.

Everything went white.

Derek opened his eyes and bolted upright.

He was in bed. In his very familiar, very normal, very *human* bedroom.

He was wearing his sleep shirt.

And he didn't have any wings.

Derek flopped back onto the bed in joyous relief. "Okay," he said, running his hands along his shoulder blades to make extra double sure there were no wings, no winglets, no sign of any wings now or ever. "It was just a dream. I'm not crazy."

He shut his eyes, willing himself back to sleep. Maybe when he woke up again, he wouldn't remember anything about the crazy tooth fairy nightmare. Everything would go back to normal.

"Just a dream," he murmured to himself as he drifted back to sleep.

But it had felt so incredibly real.

CHAPTER 5

Derek was determined not to have any more guilt-induced nightmares about tooth fairies. And that meant making up with his girlfriend. No matter what it took.

He showed up at Carly's house first thing in the morning, armed with a bouquet of her favorite flowers.

"I'm sorry," he said, as soon as she opened the door.

She looked him up and down, weighing whether this was worth her time. "For what?"

Inwardly, Derek groaned. She wanted him to read her mind and figure out exactly what he'd done to get her all riled up in the first place. "What I said last night."

She nodded slowly. "Which thing that you said?"

"All the parts that deeply offended you." Derek gave her

his best charming smile. "Okay, everything I've ever said. Or thought. Even before I met you."

She bit down on the corners of her lips. "Okay," she finally said. "You can spend some time with Randy."

Time with Randy? he thought sourly. *Sullen teenager who hates my guts?* Not exactly what he'd had in mind.

Good thing he'd come prepared.

Randy's room was dark as a cave. The walls were papered with posters of guitar-wielding rockers, and every spare surface was covered in tiny plastic figurines of aliens and spaceships. Derek didn't get it. When he was this age, his room had been filled with sports stuff. What did this kid want with a bunch of toy spaceships?

The bed was lofted, and Randy was sitting on the edge, strumming his guitar. He stopped as soon as he noticed Derek. Derek applauded, genuinely impressed. "Not bad," he said. "Didn't realize you could shred like that."

If Randy was pleased, he didn't show it. "What do *you* want?"

Derek held out his gift. He'd wrapped it that morning in old newspaper — the closest thing to wrapping paper he could find around his house. "I got you a present. Can you guess what it is?"

Randy took a long look at the hockey-stick-shaped gift. "Are you kidding?"

"No, come on," Derek urged him.

Randy rolled his eyes. "Is it a puppy?"

"No, wise guy," Derek said, ripping off the newspaper. "It's one of my hockey sticks." He grabbed a marker from Randy's desk and scrawled his name across the stick. "There. Now it's worth a lot of money."

Randy was unimpressed. "Yeah, how come you're just in the minors?" he asked. "Why don't you play in the NHL?"

Derek counted to ten. *Must not yell at Carly's kid.*

"Well, Randy, the NHL isn't all it's cracked up to be," he said, in a fakely cheery voice. "Yeah, the money's great, perks are first-class . . . but when you get caught up in that stuff, you lose what it's about."

"So what's it about?"

Good question. Hard to answer, especially when Derek's mind was spinning with memories of five-star hotels and fancy restaurants. "To me, it's about the rush of the wind as you speed across the rink, the crystal spray as your blades bite deep into the ice. I play hockey to play hockey."

He was pretty pleased with the answer.

Until Randy shot back another question. "So you can't *play hockey* in the NHL?"

Score one for Randy.

Be nice, Derek told himself. "So . . . bet you get a lot of girls with that guitar."

Randy heaved a sigh. "Can we stop this now?"

"Stop what?"

"You're just like my mom's past boyfriends," Randy complained. "You're only pretending to like me to impress her."

"You're wrong," Derek said, then waited a beat. "I'm much bigger than your mom's past boyfriends."

Randy didn't laugh. "I gotta get back to practicing." He stared pointedly down at his guitar.

Derek wondered if he'd been too hard on the kid. "Wait," Derek said. "How about you come over to my place sometime? We can jam together."

"Or how about I just go tell my mom you're actually pretty cool, and then you stop trying to bond with me?"

Derek stared at the kid, wondering if he was really as tough as he seemed. Randy stared back, stubborn and proud.

"Yeah, I'll take that deal," Derek said finally.

Hey, I tried, he told himself, retreating from the room. *Can't expect me to do any more than that.*

The whole apology thing went well enough that Carly agreed to leave the kids with a sitter and come over that night for a romantic dinner. Derek even cooked.

"You'll never believe what Randy said to me after you left," Carly said.

Uh-oh. Looked like his luck was about to run out.

"That you're 'actually pretty cool'," she said.

"Uh, yeah." Derek tried not to look relieved. "I think we made some headway."

"I'll say." Carly beamed.

Just then, Derek's cell phone vibrated with an incoming text. He glanced down at the screen:

ON 4 2 NIT. CLL ME, T

Carly saw it, too. "Who's T?"

"I have no idea."

"Sure," Carly teased.

"No, really!" Derek protested. "I'm sure it was just a wrong number." He turned back to Carly. "Okay, I need you to close your eyes. I have a surprise for you."

Carly laughed, and closed her eyes.

"Keep your eyes closed!" Derek called, heading for the kitchen. He pulled a bowl of chocolate-covered strawberries out of the fridge — Carly's favorite.

Derek carried the bowl back to the table — then froze, as a sharp pain shot through his shoulder. It felt strangely familiar.

It felt . . . like two wings had just exploded out of his back.

No, he thought in horror. *It's not possible.* But he reached behind him. Possible or not, there they were.

Wings.

"I know you're standing right in front of me," Carly said, her eyes still closed. She smiled.

"Uh . . . *keep your eyes closed!*" Derek commanded.

How could this be happening? And why *now*? Derek squeezed his eyes shut, promising himself that this was all in his imagination. When he opened his eyes, the wings would be gone.

He opened his eyes.

The wings weren't gone.

"Derek?" Carly asked.

Derek panicked. He slammed the bowl of strawberries on the table and whirled around, knocking half the plates to the floor with his wings.

"Derek?"

"Don't peek!" Derek raced for the kitchen. His clothes had already transformed themselves into a fairy uniform, complete with brightly colored tights. "I need some air!"

"What?" Carly asked, sounding concerned.

"I'm, uh, I'm not feeling well."

He heard Carly's chair scrape the floor. "Should I —"

"No!" he shouted, alarmed at the thought of her coming after him. "Can you get me some Pepto?"

As she clomped up the stairs, Derek's cell phone rang. He hurried toward the front door. As he passed the table in the entry hall, his wing slammed a huge array of hockey trophies to the floor in a deafening clatter.

"What was that?" Carly called.

"Car accident!" Derek lied. "Down the street!"

Safely outside, he ducked behind a grove of tall bushes just beyond the door. "Hello?" he whispered into the phone.

"Hey. It's me. Tracy." The voice sounded annoyed.

"Tracy who?" But Derek was afraid he knew.

"Tracy, your caseworker. Your first assignment just fell asleep. You need to get to 416 Shelter Cove."

"What?" Derek fought the urge to hurl the phone across the yard. "I thought that was a dream!"

"Think again."

Derek cursed under his breath as Carly poked her head outside the door. "Derek?"

"Bushes," Derek mumbled, diving deeper into the bushes and trying to sound sick. It wasn't too hard. "Don't come any closer. I can't let you see me like this."

"Oh, Derek, you're really sick!" He could tell that Carly was a heartbeat away from coming after him. "I can't find anything in your —"

"Try looking under the sink!" he shouted, trying to figure out what to do if he couldn't get her back into the house.

There was a long pause. "Okaaay," Carly said, drawing out the word to make it clear that she didn't approve. But she went back into the house.

Derek sighed. One problem solved.

Another one — an annoying caseworker fairy–shaped one — was still on the phone.

"You heard the rules," Tracy said. "You can't miss an assignment. Plus, those wings stay on your back until you get that tooth."

"Oh, man," Derek groaned.

Carly stuck her head out the bathroom window. "It's not under the sink!"

"Well, look in all the cabinets!" This wasn't going to work forever.

"I looked in all the cabinets. You could clean a little!"

Scratch that. This wasn't going to work for another five minutes. Derek had to make a move. *Now.* Glancing up at the window and crossing his fingers for luck, Derek sprinted into the house and grabbed his keys.

"You know what?" he shouted up to Carly. "I'm gonna take a drive, get some wind on my face. Just . . . make yourself comfortable until I get back!"

By the time Carly made it back downstairs, he was gone.

CHAPTER 6

Derek's Camaro wasn't built for wings. He felt like a turkey stuffed into a tin can. Fortunately, the address Tracy had given him wasn't very far, and it didn't take long to get there.

Unfortunately . . . the address Tracy had given him wasn't very far, and it didn't take long to get there.

Derek pulled up to the curve at the end of a cul-de-sac, grateful for the darkness of the street. He squeezed through the car's narrow doorway, hoping his wings wouldn't be permanently bent, and met Tracy in front of the house. The caseworker fairy gave him a quick once-over, then nodded his approval. "Okay, so let's go get the tooth!"

Derek didn't move. "I don't get it," he said, stalling for time. "You're a fairy, right?"

"Yeah?"

"So why don't *you* go in?"

Tracy blanched. "Because it's not my job."

"That makes no sense. Why can't you get the tooth?"

"Because I'm not a winged fairy, okay!" Tracy exclaimed. "I'm a *caseworker* fairy. It's, like, a lot more responsibility."

Derek couldn't help smiling at the fairy's defensiveness. "Ah. You mean, you're not good enough, so they stuck you at a desk?" he teased.

"There's wing discrimination, okay?" Tracy said stiffly.

Derek burst into laughter. Of all the crazy things he'd heard in the last couple days, this was the craziest.

"Oh, that's mature," Tracy said.

The fairy's sour expression just made Derek laugh all the harder. "What? I can't hear you. I have *wings* in my ears!"

Tracy slumped, with the weary acceptance of someone who'd heard it all before. "Okay. Very funny. How about you just get in the house and do your job? I think it's best if you use one power at a time."

Derek shrugged. "Maybe I'll *wing* it."

Tracy was starting to get agitated. Make that *more* agitated. "Seriously, how're you going to get in there?"

"On a *wing* and a prayer."

Tracy exploded. *"Stop fooling around and tell me how you're going to get into the house!"*

Obviously, the fairy couldn't take a joke. After everything he'd been through, Derek enjoyed watching the little guy squirm. "Which *wing* of the house do you suggest I go to first?"

Tracy balled up his fists. "You wanna get another week?"

That was enough to wipe the smile off Derek's face. "Well, I can't fly. What do *you* suggest I do?"

"How about you shrink yourself and slide under the front door?" Tracy suggested.

Derek rolled his eyes. "Oh, right. Obviously. That's what anyone would do in this situation. Shrink themselves."

But he didn't have a better plan, so he pulled the shrinking paste out of his utility pouch. It was a slim tube, like travel-sized toothpaste. Derek examined it with suspicion. "Is this gonna hurt?"

"I hope so," Tracy snapped.

"And how do I get big again?" Derek asked, worried that he'd spend the rest of his life the size of a cockroach.

"It's automatic. From the time you shrink, you start to gradually regrow. Usually takes about an hour. Ready?"

Not even a little bit.

"Oh, man," Derek groaned. He squeezed the shrinking paste into his mouth. It tasted like mint-flavored mold.

Nothing happened.

And then the world exploded around him, like

everything had suddenly been supersized. He felt like he was falling, very far and very fast. Everything loomed over him: the houses. The cars. Even the uncut grass, bowing in the wind like giant cornstalks. Derek suspected that if he took a wrong turn, he'd be lost forever. At least until he got eaten by a squirrel.

Tracy was a giant, towering hundreds of feet high. He raised a massive, truck-sized foot and dangled it over Derek's puny head. "No!" Mini-Derek chirped. "Please don't hurt me! Please!"

"I know you're talking, little man." Tracy's voice was thunder in Derek's ears. "But I can't hear you with that little-man voice." His giant foot returned to the ground without squashing Derek into a puddle of tooth fairy mush.

"Yeah, well, I'm not going to be a little man for long," Derek said, hoping he sounded tougher than he felt. "Once I'm big, you'll be sorry."

"Is the little bitty tiny man getting mad?" Tracy teased in baby talk. He leaned down, and his gigantic face filled Derek's field of vision. Derek resisted the urge to poke his caseworker in the eye. "Here," Tracy said, shoving a dollar bill at Derek. The thing was as big as a carpet, and just as heavy.

Better get this over with, Derek thought. He rolled under the door and, with a mighty tug, yanked the dollar bill through after him.

The hallway was a funhouse of distorted shapes. A pile of shoes the size of a mountain. A table with legs as thick as tree trunks. A stuffed mouse with a painted red mouth as big as Derek's head.

A loud wheezing noise cut through the silence.

Derek froze. He looked again at the mouse, his brain spinning. Where there were toy mice, there was all too often —

A CAT!

Goosebumps covered Derek's arms, and the hair on the back of his neck jumped to attention. Curled into a slumbering mound, the massive cat seemed like a dinosaur. Derek was barely the size of one of its paws, each of which bore sharp claws that could surely tear him in two. Its furry chest rose and fell in even, labored breaths. It was asleep.

For now.

Derek held his breath and tiptoed past the monster, slipping into the first room he came to. Judging from the giant soccer ball and the stuffed alligator — big enough to swallow him whole — he'd found the right spot. Now all he needed to do was grab the tooth and get out.

Unfortunately, the tooth was under the kid's pillow. And the kid's pillow was on the kid's bed. Which might as well have been a mile high, as far as Derek was concerned.

But he hadn't come this far to give up.

Next to the bed, there was a dresser. Its lowest drawer handle jutted out just above Derek's head. He rolled up the dollar bill and stuck it down the back of his shirt, like an archery quiver. Then he took a running leap and grabbed the handle, hoisting himself up. The kid's comforter hung over the edge of the bed, only a couple arm lengths away.

Here goes nothing, Derek thought.

He launched himself off the drawer handle. For a brief second, he was flying — and then he slammed into the side of the bed. He flailed wildly, grabbing two fistfuls of comforter just before he slipped to the ground. Now it was just a matter of climbing. Slowly, painfully, he dragged himself up the side of the comforter, one hand after another. Finally, he was on top of the bed, face to face with a sleeping child.

The kid was several times larger than the cat — but somehow, he was also less terrifying. Maybe it was the look on his face as he slept, the way his mouth curled up into a smile, like he was having a particularly good dream. *Just keep sleeping*, Derek silently urged him as he tiptoed past the child's face and wiggled under the pillow. *Trust me, it'll be better for both of us.*

There it was, squarely under the pillow: the tooth! It was slightly soggy and a little larger than a pumpkin to miniature Derek. Derek slid the dollar bill under the pillow and tiptoed back toward the edge of the bed. He hesitated, wondering how to get down without dropping the bulky tooth.

The kid solved the problem for him. He turned over in his sleep — and sent Derek flying.

"Waaaaaaaaah!" Derek screamed as he plummeted toward the floor. It came at him fast, too fast, and he braced for a bone-breaking landing . . . but instead he landed with a soft *whoosh* right on top of the stuffed alligator. The kid's eyes flew open at the sound of Derek's scream, and he peered over the edge of the bed.

Then *he* started to scream.

Derek panicked. He ran for the door, but he was too slow. Before Derek could escape, the kid's parents burst into the room. Derek flattened himself against the bedroom wall . . . just in time for the bedroom door to smash him flat.

"What happened?" a woman's voice asked, as Derek peeled himself off the wall. "What's the matter?"

"I saw a tiny man," the kid wailed.

This was his chance, Derek decided. No one would notice if he tiptoed out of the room and down the hall . . . no one except the cat.

The hairy monster stood in the center of the hall, hissing evilly. Its teeth gleamed in the dark, and its eyes glowed a sinister orange. There was no way Derek would be fast enough to get past it, not without getting shish-kebabed by one of those razor-sharp fangs.

Derek searched for something that could help him escape. His eyes rested on a pile of junk heaped at the edge of the kid's room. Lying on top was a doll-sized toy skateboard — and there was a miniature half-pipe only a few inches away. It was perfect . . . except for the fact that Derek didn't know how to ride a skateboard.

Time to learn, he thought. *Fast.*

Derek grabbed the skateboard off the pile and balanced on the edge of the curved ramp. He wobbled for a moment, then caught his balance. And, with a mighty push, he launched himself onto the half-pipe as hard as he could. The skateboard skidded across the ramp at top speed, then caught air. He was flying! Out of the bedroom, over the cat, down the hall . . . and then he was falling.

Totally out of control, Derek threw himself off the skateboard as it slammed into the floor. The cat was already after him, hissing and mewing. Derek sped down the hall and veered around a corner, ducking into the kitchen. He clung to a giant table leg and held his breath. The cat nosed its way into the room, looking confused. Its nose twitched. It was only a matter of time before the creature sniffed him out — and chowed down.

Derek fumbled in his utility pouch and grabbed his magic wand, remembering the All-Purpose Magic Generator Button. He took a deep breath, aimed the wand at the cat . . . and pressed the button.

Nothing happened, not even a sputter. And the cat was getting closer. Derek reached deeper into the pouch and found something he'd forgotten was there, a tiny bottle marked "Cat-Away." There was a miniature horn on top. At his size, Derek had little hope that the bottle would scare away a flea, much less a cat. But he pressed the button.

AAAAAAAAOOOOOOOOOOOOOO!

The cat leapt several feet in the air, spooked by the loudest horn Derek had ever heard. His ears ringing, he raced past the stunned cat, flinging himself through the cat flap in the front door. *Freedom!* He didn't stop until he'd powered his way across the lawn, down the sidewalk, and smack into Tracy's waiting hand.

The caseworker fairy scooped him off the ground, peering down at Derek's tiny form, his lips curled into a satisfied smirk. "Want a lift to your car?"

*　　*　　*

When Derek got home, Carly was asleep on the couch. That was lucky, since the shrinking paste hadn't worn off. He was still only a couple feet tall! Derek tiptoed past her, planning to lock himself in the bedroom until he was normal size again.

"Derek . . ." Carly mumbled, half asleep.

Derek darted behind the couch. "Carly!" The word slipped out before he could stop himself. His voice sounded like he'd sucked down half a tank of helium.

"What?" Carly started to sit up.

"Goin' to bed," Derek said quickly, heading across the room as quickly as his little legs would carry him.

"What happened to you?" Carly called, as he hit the stairs. "I was worried."

Each stair was half as tall as he was, but Derek pulled himself up, one by one. "I might still have whatever it was that I had!" Derek called back, cringing at his crazy voice.

"Whatever," Carly said flatly.

He sighed. She probably knew he was lying to her. But there was nothing he could do until he cleaned up this tooth fairy mess. After things got back to normal, he'd make it up to her, he promised himself.

Assuming things were ever normal again.

CHAPTER 7

Usually, Ice Wolves hockey games were covered on local radio — that is, when they were covered at all. But this game was different. ESPN was broadcasting live from the ice. Derek had been excited . . . until he heard the promos. They were filled with nauseating bluster about "Mick Donnelly's historic professional hockey debut!" and "Mick Donnelly, the Canadian phenom!" Not to mention, "Mick Donnelly, the next Great One." Derek told himself not to let the radio stooges bother him. Soon they'd understand what every Ice Wolves fan already knew: Derek *was* the Ice Wolves. If anyone was going to be the next Great One, it was him.

Derek and Mick were the last to leave the locker room. "So, kid, you pumped for your first game?" Derek asked, remembering his first professional game. He'd been so nervous, he'd nearly thrown up behind the arena.

"Yeah, Pa," Mick snarled. "I'm super pumped because it just means one less game till I'm bumped on out of here and up to the bigs."

Derek lost what little patience he had left. It had been a long, horrible week — but now they were on *his* turf, *his* ice, and there was no way he was going to let some snot-nosed, air-headed, overrated kid treat him like yesterday's news.

"You know what? I'm done being generous. You're in *my* kingdom now." He gave Mick a light shove, just to let him know who was boss. "I'm the king and you're not even a prince. You're like one of those guys who wanders around the court in tights and a poofy wig."

The stands were full, but there wasn't a single Tooth Fairy banner to be seen.

"*Mick the Stick!*" the fans roared, as he stepped onto the ice. "*Mick the Stick! Mick the Stick!*"

Mick cocked an eyebrow at Derek. "Looks like you've been dethroned."

One minute to go in the last period, and the Ice Wolves were leading the Storm two to one. Mick was working on a hat trick — three goals in one game. The puck skidded into the Ice Wolves' zone. Two burly members of the Storm chased after it. Mick threw himself into the fray and smacked the puck out of their reach. He started racing across the ice, but the Storm triple-teamed him, blocking his path to the goal.

Derek charged into the fray, eager to knock out a few defensemen. And, if he did his job right, maybe a few teeth.

He waited to hear the crowd roaring his nickname, but *"Mick the Stick!"* still echoed through the arena. No matter. Derek barreled toward the scrum of players, head down, ready to knock some helmets together.

But then he felt that all-too-familiar jolt across his shoulder blades.

And he fell flat on his face.

Now the crowd noticed him — just in time to start booing.

With Derek down, there was no one to block for Donnelly. Left defenseless, he got slammed into the boards. The Storm snagged the puck and shot it down the ice, just as the light on the scoreboard flared. Game over.

Derek needed to get off the ice before he sprouted wings, but first he had to maneuver through the wall of angry fans.

"Tooth Fairy stinks," one of them snarled, glaring as he shuffled past. "My little baby girl could do better out there."

"What makes you think you can skate?" another taunted. "Why don't you do us all a favor and retire!"

Derek had never messed up a game so badly. He just wanted to slink off and hide, but the coach blocked his path. "What happened out there, Thompson?"

Before he could come up with an answer, Derek was distracted by the scoreboard. Instead of the final score, it was flashing a message: KID'S ASLEEP @ 2631 CASTLE HEIGHTS.

"No," Derek said, disgusted.

"What's the *matter* with you?" the coach growled.

"It's kinda complicated. Sorry, gotta go, Coach." He squeezed his way around the coach.

"If you can't do your job, I'll find someone else who will!" the coach called after him. But Derek was already halfway through the tunnel that led to the locker room. He had bigger problems to deal with.

Mick was on him the moment he stepped into the locker room. "Hey, Thompson, you just cost me a hat trick and an interview on ESPN —"

Ignoring him, Derek hurried straight to the bathroom stalls. He slammed the door behind him just in time. Wings sprouted through his uniform, which was already beginning to transform itself into full-on fairy gear.

"Get out here!" Mick shouted, banging on the stall door. "I want to talk to you!"

The Lansing Ice Wolves hockey team only needed one thing to win: The Tooth Fairy.

Derek Thompson earned that nickname by being a hard-hitter on the ice. He smashed into his opponents so hard that he knocked their teeth out!

But when young Mick Donnelly joined the team, Derek wasn't the star anymore. Derek was angry and ready to give up.

Derek forgot to put tooth fairy money under his girlfriend's daughter, Tess's, pillow, and even tried to tell her there was no such thing as the tooth fairy.

But he never expected to wake up that night with wings! As punishment for what he'd done, Derek had been turned into a real, live tooth fairy.

Derek was given magical fairy supplies and was put through flight training. But when he woke up in his own bed the next morning, the wings came back.

That night, Derek went on his first tooth fairy mission. He had to use shrinking paste to make himself tiny so he could sneak under doors!

Fed up, he barged into the next house without even trying to hide.

Lily, the head of the tooth fairies, wasn't happy with Derek's behavior. She gave him many more assignments to do!

Unfortunately, those didn't go so well, either.

But when Derek put his mind to it, he was a pretty decent tooth fairy. He even came up with a cool costume.

Things began going better for Derek on the ice, too.

Finally, he made up with his girlfriend and her kids. He got her son, Randy, a brand-new guitar for his talent show. And he helped Tess believe in the tooth fairy again!

But most importantly, Derek learned that against all odds, sometimes dreams do come true.

"Sorry, no autographs right now," Derek said in a strained voice. "Little busy."

But Mick wasn't going anywhere. "Fine. I'll wait, Thompson."

Moments later, Derek heard a few more of the players come in. A big hulk named Andreas peered under the door of the stall, catching site of Derek's fairy slippers.

Great, thought Derek, as the rest of the guys started chattering about his footwear. *I'll never live this one down.*

"Check out Thompson's shoes!"

"There's a lady in the men's bathroom!"

They started pounding on the door. It wouldn't hold for long. In desperation, Derek yanked out his wand and pushed the big red button. "Disappear!" he shouted. But the wand was still a dud.

"Oh, no," Mick said angrily. "Either you come out, or we're bustin' in. On . . . *one* . . . !"

Derek looked around the stall. There were only two ways out. Either through the door or . . .

He stared down at the toilet, crusted with layers of gunk. The banging on the door got louder. Running out of options, Derek squeezed a dab of shrinking paste into his mouth. Then he climbed onto the edge of the toilet bowl, and flushed.

"*Two!*" the Ice Wolves shouted.

A six-inch-high Derek stood on the toilet bowl, staring down at the whirling cesspool. He clamped his lips shut, pinched his nose together, and cannonballed into the water.

"*Three!*" The door burst open as half the team burst into the stall, just as the freshly flushed toilet water swirled down the drain . . . taking Derek with it.

"Where were you?" Tracy asked impatiently when Derek finally showed up at the squat house at 2631 Castle Heights. "You're late. Why are you all wet?"

Derek fumed. His hair was dripping in his face. His fairy costume was soaked and sticking to his damp body. He smelled like a sewer. And every time he closed his eyes, he heard that thunderous flushing sound, saw the whirlpool that had sucked him down into a nightmare of sludge and —

No. At that very moment, Derek decided never to think about that little water ride ever again.

"Oh, jeeeeez!" Tracy exclaimed, catching a whiff of Derek's foul stench.

"Don't talk to me!" Derek shouted, rushing past him to the front door of the house. "I hate this job." He didn't bother to form a plan. He wouldn't be using shrinking paste any time soon. And he was in *no* mood for giant cats. He just wanted to get in, get the tooth, and get out. The faster this went, the sooner he could get out of the sludge-covered uniform and into a scalding hot shower.

He rang the doorbell. Then pressed it again. Finally, a man came to the door. "Hi," Derek said, irritably. The man opened his mouth to speak, but Derek flung a puff of amnesia dust into his face, then pushed past him.

"Hank?" A woman asked, stepping into the entryway. "Who's at the —" Her eyes widened when she saw Derek, in full fairy gear. "What is —?"

A handful of amnesia dust took care of her, too. "Nice to meet you," Derek said politely, then ventured deeper into the house. Like a video game, it was filled with obstacles: brothers, sisters, a hunched-over old lady, a rambunctious puppy. . . . But Derek didn't let any of them stop him, even for a moment. The amnesia dust took care of them all. *A little amnesia dust a day keeps the grannies away*, Derek thought, as he blew a pinch in the old woman's face.

The kid's bedroom was at the end of the hall. She was curled up in bed, asleep.

Not for long, Derek thought.

He yanked the pillow out from under her and flung a crumpled handful of bills at the mattress. Then he scooped up the tooth and stuffed it in his pocket. The little girl gaped up at him, but a little amnesia dust turned her expression from surprise to confusion. "Have a nice day," Derek said cheerfully, and booked it out of the house.

Five minutes flat, he thought, rather proud of himself. *Not too shabby.*

That's when the night ripped open and Derek was flung off his feet, sucked into a swirling vortex.

Everything went white.

The vortex dumped Derek smack into Lily's office, up in fairy central. She sneered at him from behind her desk. Tracy fidgeted beside her, looking like he wished he had some dust that would make them all disappear.

Derek knew why he was there — and he didn't care. "Here's your tooth," he said, tossing it at Lily. "Enjoy doing whatever you do with it."

She raised her hand, and the tooth shifted course in midair to land squarely in her palm.

Not possible, Derek thought, rubbing his eyes. But then he remembered where he was, and that he had wings sprouting out of his back and a defective magic wand tucked into his utility belt. These days, anything was possible.

Lily placed the tooth on her desk. "Derek, according to your caseworker, you're not exactly embracing the tooth fairy spirit."

Derek glared at Tracy. Tattletale. "Yeah, well, I think my

caseworker has some serious wing envy." He leaned toward Lily. "Feels discriminated against. Hope he doesn't sue."

"I didn't say that!" Tracy yelped. "I'm completely and totally happy administrating and wouldn't wish to be doing anything else."

Derek shook his head sadly. "Denial. Not pretty."

Tracy's eyes were bulging again. "Listen, this guy's got wings and doesn't even care."

Lily was clearly too polite to roll her eyes, but her weary disdain was evident in her voice. "I didn't call you two in here to argue in front of me." She flicked her fingers, and a giant screen descended from the ceiling. "Look what you did to that family!"

The screen lit up with the people he'd dosed with amnesia dust. They bumbled around the living room, staring at each other in horror. "Who are you?" the father asked.

"Who are *you*?" the mother shot back accusingly.

"I don't know!"

"Know what?"

Meanwhile, the grandmother was spinning in slow, aimless circles. "Where am I?"

"They've been at this for *hours*," Lily complained.

Derek shot her a sheepish grin. "I thought it would wear off."

Lily scowled. "Eventually. But you overdid it."

Glancing back at the screen, Derek had to admit that maybe he had. But how was that *his* fault? They were the ones who'd sent him into the field without knowing what he was doing!

Derek suddenly realized he might be onto something. "Do *you* have a supervisor?" he asked Lily. "Like — I don't know — Gandhi? Because I'd like to file a complaint."

Lily wasn't even listening. One of her assistants had poked his head into the office and handed her a slip of paper. She raised her eyebrows at Derek. "You have another assignment."

That stopped him cold. "*What?* Another lost tooth?"

She shrugged. "Some nights there're no assignments. Some nights there's a doubleheader."

Arguing would just waste more time. "Well, where is it?" Derek asked. "I want to take care of it and go home."

Lily shook her head with the ghost of a smile. "Not until the child falls asleep. Until then, you need to wait."

The smile grew wider. She was *enjoying* this.

Tracy gripped Derek's arm and escorted him to a cramped little waiting room, where they were stuck until the kid's bedtime.

The waiting room was like any other waiting room Derek had ever been stuck in. Vending machines lined the walls, empty Styrofoam cups littered the floor, scratchy Muzak pumped through the ancient speakers, and dog-eared magazines littered the side tables. Derek riffled through them, hoping for a copy of *Inside Hockey* or at least a *Sports Illustrated*. Instead, he was stuck with *Fairy Men's Health*.

With a disgusted sigh, Derek slumped down in one of the uncomfortable, hard-backed chairs. He opened the magazine to a random page and ran his eyes over the text, barely absorbing any of "Stronger Wings in 8 Quick Weeks." He'd didn't need the tips; he'd be done with all this long before eight weeks.

He hoped.

A gaggle of babbling fairies burst into the room, chattering about their night's work. They veered straight for the water cooler. "I just got my wings waxed," one of them confided loudly to his friends, shooting Tracy a nasty look. "It really gives you a lot more speed."

"Does it hurt?" another asked.

The fairy shrugged, fluffing his wings like a peacock. "Just a little. But it's worth it."

Tracy gazed longingly at the fairies' magnificent wings. A faint red flush crept up his face when he caught Derek watching him. Feeling almost bad for the guy, Derek looked away.

Derek read the magazine straight through, cover to cover.

Next came *Vanity Fairy*. Then *Working Fairy*.

And, in desperation, *Fairy Women's Wear Weekly*.

He began to wonder whether someone had slipped him some magical time-stretching dust, because every minute was taking an eternity. The other fairies in the room slipped away. Even Tracy yawned and headed off to wherever fairy caseworkers go when they're off the clock.

Derek stretched out on a row of chairs, exhausted. He closed his eyes and tried to ignore the edge of the chair digging into his hip, the annoying whine of the vending machines, and most especially, the sour, rotten smell oozing from his sewer-drenched pores. It took a full hour of lying there motionless, eyes squeezed shut, counting enemies, but he finally drifted off somewhere between Lily and Mick Donnelly. (In Derek's drowsy, wandering mind, Donnelly was dressed as a fairy with pink glittering wings, while Lily glided across the ice in heavy Ice Wolves padding, stick lofted for a major slap shot.)

Just when he'd gotten to sleep, the loud buzz of his cell phone snapped him wide awake. It was an incoming text message:

Assignment cancelled.

CHAPTER 8

Derek would have been happy to sleep forever. And he definitely would have been happy to sleep past nine A.M., which was when a blaring horn jolted him awake.

He rolled over and shoved his head under a pillow. But the pillow did little to muffle the noise. Eventually, Derek dragged himself out of bed, shrugged on a bathrobe, and stumbled out to the balcony. Then he leaned over the railing, ready to tell whoever it was to leave him alone.

But it was Carly.

"Hi!" she shouted up at him, leaning against her car. "You feeling any better?"

All at once, Derek was wide awake. Seeing Carly was perhaps the only thing that could wash away the memory of his horrible night. "Yes, I am," he called down to her. "Come on in!"

"Well, actually, I need a huge favor," Carly admitted. Tess peeked out of the passenger's side window and waved up at Derek. "Tess and I just got a last-minute invite to a —"

"Beauty makeover party!" Tess shouted.

Derek groaned inwardly. Much as he liked hanging out with Carly and her kid, a beauty makeover party wasn't *exactly* the day he'd had in mind.

"Since you and Randy are hitting it off so well now, I was hoping he could hang out with you while we go?" Carly asked.

Randy climbed out of the car, shooting Derek a look that was half sullen, half sheepish. So much for their brilliant plan.

"Uh, yeah," Derek said, like he had any other choice. "Sure. It'll give us a chance to bond some more."

Randy just stared at the ground.

"I'll make it up to you. I promise." Carly blew Derek a kiss. "Be good," she reminded Randy before speeding away. "Have fun, you two!"

It didn't seem likely.

Just wait him out, Derek told himself as Randy stood sullenly in the doorway. *He'll have to talk eventually.* Randy glanced at the peeling paint, the fraying rug, the ratty furniture, the cluttered trophy shelves. "I can see hockey's been really good to you," he said dryly.

"You want to hang with me?" Derek said, a warning note in his voice. "Or you want to get a beauty makeover?"

Randy didn't dignify that one with an answer.

Derek sighed. "All right. What do you say we go outside and shoot some hoops?"

The kid just glared.

"Throw a football?" Derek tried again.

Randy's eyebrows knit together in an angry V.

"Batting cages?" Derek said.

That earned him Randy's coldest stare yet.

"Okay, fine." There had to be *something* out there the kid didn't hate. Derek thought for a moment — then he had it. The perfect plan. "How about something indoors?"

Randy didn't object when Derek ushered him out of the apartment and into the blue Camaro. He just stared out the window. But when they pulled up in front of the store, a giant neon guitar twirling overhead, Derek was sure he caught a very tiny, very brief, very real smile.

Inside, speakers pumped a loud guitar riff throughout the store. Derek and Randy passed racks of sheet music, shelves lined with amps, a huge display of high-end strings, and a vintage Les Paul encased behind glass. Randy took it all in, mouth open, eyes glassy. As they approached the display of electric guitars, Derek did a double take. Was Randy actually *smiling*?

"Whattya think?" Derek said. "Nice stuff, huh?"

A pack of teenagers came into the store, their loud voices mixing in with the music. Randy flushed and stepped behind one of the large display shelves. "Yeah. Whatever."

"Why don't you pick one up and play a little?" Derek urged him.

"No, I don't want to."

"No, man, seriously. Try one."

But Randy just stood there, hands shoved in his pockets, looking as bored and cranky as ever. Frustrated, Derek resolved to shake him out of it.

He took a good look at the shelf. He didn't know that much about guitars, but he knew cool. And the vintage Fender Stratocaster, its frets black as midnight against a silver neck, its body a deep blue, was definitely cool. He grabbed the guitar and held it out to Randy. "Go ahead."

While Derek plugged it into an amp, Randy stayed frozen, staring down at the guitar like he didn't know how it had gotten there.

"Let's hear what it sounds like," Derek urged him.

Randy didn't move.

Derek threw up his hands. "Sounds great," he drawled, defeated. "I'm gonna go check out some drums and sticks. I'll be back. You just . . . keep practicing." He walked away — but he'd barely turned the corner when he heard quiet guitar strumming come from Randy's aisle. Derek nodded in satisfaction. So the kid was human after all. He paused, pretending to test out some of the drumsticks, but really he was listening to Randy play. Then the sound cut off abruptly.

"Hi, Randy." It was a girl's voice.

Derek knew he probably shouldn't be eavesdropping. But he did it anyway.

"Oh, hey, what's up?" Randy said. Derek barely recognized the voice. Randy never sounded so light and friendly when he spoke to Derek. He also never sounded so nervous.

"Was that you playing?" the girl asked.

A pause. "Yeah. I guess."

Don't sound so modest, kid, Derek urged him silently. *Own it.*

"Sounds pretty good," the girl said.

"Thanks."

Derek could almost hear the blush in his voice.

"Are you gonna play in the talent show?" she asked.

A meathead teenager in an ugly football jacket pushed

past Derek. He rounded the corner into Randy's aisle. "Kelly?" he said, sounding none too pleased. "There you are. Why are you talking to emo boy?"

Derek bristled. Who *was* this kid? He waited for Randy to stick up for himself, but . . . nothing.

"Don't be a jerk, Ben," the girl said.

"Your dad's waiting," Ben told her. "We gotta go."

"Bye, Randy!" the girl said. Randy didn't answer.

Derek heard the girl scamper away. But Ben stayed behind. "Don't even *think* about talking to her. Got it, loser?"

"Okay," Randy mumbled.

Derek had had enough. He rounded the aisle just in time to see Ben grab the guitar out of Randy's hand. "And you really should put this back, 'cause you stink," Ben growled.

Enough, Derek thought. He crept up behind Ben and rapped his drumsticks on the kid's head. "Hey, nice hollow sound."

Ben turned around, and looked up at Derek.

Way up. Ben may have been big for a teenager, but he was still a teenager. And Derek was a professional hockey player who knocked out guys' teeth for a living. "You play, little man?" Derek said innocently.

"No, sir," Ben said, his face slightly pale.

"Then what are you doing with Randy's guitar?"

Ben looked down at the guitar. "Ummm, nothing?"

"Why don't you give it back?"

Ben nodded eagerly. Anything to get away from the giant who could break him in two. "Okay." He handed Randy the guitar, who was trying not to smile.

"Tell him you're sorry," Derek commanded.

"I'm sorry," Ben muttered.

"Now tell him *why* you're sorry."

"I'm sorry because I grabbed the guitar," Ben groveled.

"And?" Derek said.

"And . . . it was really insensitive of me?"

Derek glanced at Randy. "Do you accept his apology?"

Randy pretended to think about it. "Yeah."

Derek grinned. "Get out of here."

Ben left the store as fast as he could. He probably didn't want to look like a coward and actually *run* away, but his crazy power walk made him look like some kind of over-caffeinated duck.

Randy shot Derek a grateful smile. Maybe this whole bonding thing could work after all.

"So, can you beat two pair?" Derek asked, peering at Randy over his hand of cards. The kid had only learned how to play that afternoon, but his stash of Cheez Doodles was twice the size of Derek's.

"Call me and find out," Randy said good-naturedly.

Since they'd come home from the guitar store, he'd been like a different person.

Derek tossed his cards on the table. "Aces over kings," he boasted, surprised to realize he was actually having fun.

The corners of Randy's lips turned up. He laid his cards down one by one. A six of clubs, a seven of clubs, an eight of clubs . . .

Derek started to get a bad feeling.

Slowly, Randy laid down the final two cards — a nine and ten of clubs. "Straight flush," he said, with false modesty.

"No way!"

Randy scooped the pot of Cheez Doodles into his massive pile. He began playing with the little orange puffs, building them into an elaborate heap. He chewed on the corner of his lip for a moment. "Can I ask you a question?"

Derek took a deep breath. Uh-oh. "What is it?"

Randy shrugged, as if to make clear that whatever it was, it was no big deal. A dead giveaway that it was a *very* big deal. "There's this talent show coming up at my school, and my mom thinks I should play in it. But . . . I don't know."

"Well, maybe you *should* play in it."

Randy shifted in his seat. It seemed like he was gearing up to explain. But they were interrupted by a knock at the door.

"We're back!" Carly called, using her key to enter.

Randy clammed up.

"We're up here!" Derek said, surprised to discover that he was a little disappointed.

Carly had Tess in tow. Both were caked in garish makeup, their hair sprayed stiff and puffed up about six inches from their heads. Carly still managed to look gorgeous, of course. Tess just looked ridiculous.

"Hey, boys, how'd it go?" Carly asked.

"Your boy cheats at cards," Derek teased. "And you look, uh . . ."

"Gorgeeeeeouuuuuus!" Tess cried proudly.

"Took the word right out of my mouth."

Carly laughed, looking pleasantly surprised to discover Randy and Derek were both still breathing. "You guys hungry?" she asked. "Maybe we should all go out to dinner?"

"Sure," Derek said. "Sounds great —" His cell phone buzzed. He broke out in a cold sweat and, for a brief moment, considered ignoring it. But he knew what would happen if he did. He snuck a glance at the screen: **436 Cottsville Rd. Now**. "Or maybe some other time," he said quickly, eager to get them out of his house before his wings showed up.

"Why?" Carly asked. She looked pointedly at the phone. "What's that?"

Derek stuffed the phone into his pocket. "Nothing. Just a . . . an emergency."

"A *hockey* emergency?" She sounded dubious.

"Yes, actually." Derek steered her toward the door. The kids trailed after them. "Sorry, guys. I'll call you later."

"Is someone hurt?" Carly asked, standing in the doorway. He could feel the prickly heat spreading across his shoulder blades. Any minute now, the situation was going to get completely out of control.

"Yes," Derek said, thinking it would be easiest. He realized his mistake as soon as Carly opened her mouth, clearly eager to help. "No!" he corrected himself awkwardly. She knew he was lying — even *Tess* probably knew he was lying. But what else could he do? "Not in a way that you need to be worried at all. Sprained wrist! I'll call you tomorrow." He practically pushed the three of them outside and slammed the door behind them.

The last thing he saw was the expression on Randy's face, a mixture of suspicion and disappointment. And, worst of all, a weary lack of surprise, as if Derek had just lived down to his expectations.

What else is new? Derek thought gloomily. Then he grabbed his wand and got to work.

CHAPTER 9

Shrinking paste?" Derek mumbled, searching through his tool kit for something that might get the job done. "No, not that again. Amnesia dust — *no*. Flying?" He had a nasty flashback to his disastrous efforts in the flight training center. "Forget it. Oh, and my All-Purpose Magic Generator Button?" He shook the useless magic wand, tempted to break it in two. "Doesn't work. Broken."

Tracy was watching him, arms crossed, toe tapping impatiently. "Why don't you try invisibility?" he suggested.

That would have been my next idea, Derek assured himself. He had to admit it was a good one. The spray came in a tiny aerosol can. He gave it a hard shake, then sprayed it all over himself. It smelled like Lysol.

Several moments passed, and nothing happened.

"And . . . it's not really working," Derek complained. "What a surprise. You guys need better quality control."

Then he looked down at his hands. Or, at least, where his hands should have been. But there was nothing but thin air. He checked the rest of himself — totally invisible.

"If only it could last forever," Tracy grumbled.

"I heard that," Derek snapped. He was invisible, not deaf.

It was strange to hear his voice floating in the air. It was the only evidence Derek had that he still existed. Well, that and the ghostly footprints he tracked through the mud as he headed for the house.

This one was larger than the others he'd visited — not quite a mansion, but definitely bigger than *his* place. He slipped inside without any trouble, easing the door shut behind him. Then he tiptoed through the entry hall and into the living room. The carpeting was plush, and Derek was pretty confident he could make it across without a sound. He would have to, since the kid's parents were sitting on a couch in the middle of the room, watching TV.

He crept safely across the room, snuck into the kid's bedroom, and made the switch. By the time he made it back to the living room with the tooth, he was feeling pretty impressed with himself. And then his left wing slammed into one of the bookshelves and sent a family of glass elephants crashing to the floor.

Derek froze. Across the house, a dog began to bark.

The clueless couple exchanged a glance. "Earthquake?" the wife wondered.

Derek risked another step, brushing against a book and knocking it toward the floor. He lunged forward, catching it just before it fell — and, in the process, knocked a collection of antique teapots to the ground in a noisy clatter.

"Ghosts!" the wife cried in alarm. She clutched her husband's arm.

They wanted a ghost? He'd give them a ghost.

"Boo," he said, experimentally.

The woman screamed. Her husband put an arm around her. "Let's stay calm, honey. Maybe it's a benign spirit." He turned toward the bookshelf, staring about three feet to the left of Derek. "Are you lost? Can we help you?"

His wife chimed in. "Are YOU . . . FROM . . . HERE?"

This was fun, but Derek didn't have all night. He pulled out his amnesia dust and got ready to toss a handful toward the couple. But that was easier said than done when you were invisible. He couldn't figure out where his tool kit was — he could barely figure out where his hand was. Which is how he managed to toss the dust directly in his own face.

After that, things got confusing.

What am I doing? Derek thought. *Where am I?* He looked around the strange living room, with a strange couple sitting on the couch. The woman's eyes bugged out and then, with a little scream and shudder, she passed out. The man's hand shook as he lifted the phone and, with a trembling finger, dialed 911. Then Derek looked down at himself and realized there was nothing there.

"Just go to the white light, my friend," the man said nervously. "The white light . . ."

Derek had no idea what was going on, so he figured it was probably best to do what he was told. He walked toward the closest light he could find.

"That's a lamp!" the man shouted.

New plan, Derek thought. *Wherever I am, maybe it's time to get out.*

He headed for what looked like the front door. Just as he was about to turn the knob and escape, he heard a deep-throated growling behind him. And he made one final mistake: He looked back.

An angry brown terrier launched itself off the ground and leapt straight at Derek, fangs first. *I'm invisible*, Derek thought hopefully, as the tiny, yapping ball of rage flew toward his face. *Maybe the dog will sail right through me.*

It didn't.

"What is this?" Lily asked irritably. "Where's the tooth?"

Derek couldn't believe it. *She* was angry? *He* was the one with a giant lump on his head, a chewed-up fairy uniform, and a very confused dog hanging from his wing. And Lily had whisked him up to fairyland to complain about a missing *tooth?*

He pulled the tooth out of his pocket and dropped it into Lily's waiting palm.

She shook her head. "You just might be the worst tooth fairy ever."

"When will you know for sure?"

Maybe then they would finally fire him.

"Oh," he added quickly, before she kicked him out of the office. "I'm running low. I need more stuff."

Lily raised an eyebrow. *"Stuff?"*

"Yeah. The magic stuff. I'm out."

"Those supplies were supposed to last you the whole week," Lily pointed out.

And I was supposed *to be hanging out with Carly and the kids tonight*, he thought sourly. *Stuff happens.* "Well, they didn't."

"No," Lily said abruptly. "No more supplies."

"Oh, that's brilliant," he snapped. "I've got a week and a half to go. How am I supposed to do my job?" It was like they *wanted* him to fail.

That's it, he realized. Why else would they send him on these ridiculous missions when it was clear he had no idea what he was doing? They probably watched on Lily's big screen, laughing and chowing down on popcorn while he got his face nibbled off by hungry puppies.

"I'm sorry," Lily said. It was the most sincere-sounding apology he'd ever heard from her. Which wasn't saying much. "We're running very low on funding. And would you like to know why?"

"Not really."

"Because kids aren't *believing* like they used to." Lily was looking past him, into the distance, her gaze foggy and sorrowful. "And it's not just us. Unicorns, leprechauns, dragons. All those departments — gone. And you know why this is happening?" She didn't pause long enough for him to answer. "Because of people like you!"

"And this is a problem why?" Derek asked. Leprechauns had always seemed kind of creepy to him. And who needed dragons, anyway?

"Because if the trend continues, tooth fairyland will cease to exist. And no child will ever again receive a visit from the tooth fairy. Ever."

"So what?" If nothing else, that would solve Derek's problems. And as far as he could see, the fairies weren't doing much good for anyone else, either.

"You *really* don't see the value in what we do?" Lily asked, incredulous.

"Pay close attention to my head." Derek shook it slowly, back and forth. No, no, *no*.

"You don't see that a child's ability to imagine is important? That it's the basis for their ability to dream?"

Derek had dreams, once. He'd had dreams of playing professional hockey. Of doing interviews on CNN. Of lounging in his palatial mansion. He'd dreamed of leading his team to the Stanley Cup. And what had his dreams gotten him? A busted shoulder, a gas-guzzling car, and a position on a puny minor league team. He didn't score. He didn't steal the puck. He barely even played hockey — what he did was shove guys out of the way and knock out their teeth. He might as well be the team mascot. All thanks to his dreams. "Dreams are bad," he said firmly, and meant it.

Lily could barely look at him. "You're done."

Derek felt a stab of hope. "For the week?"

"No. For the night. Unless you feel like staying for fairy-okee."

It took him a minute to figure out what she was talking about. Then he got it. Not *fairy-okee*. *Fairaoke.* Like *karaoke.* "And I thought there was nothing worse than regular karaoke," he muttered, hurrying out of the office.

He was quickly lost in the maze of corridors. Soon he found himself in a hallway with a busted light. A sleazy fairy lurked in the shadows, his uniform tattered, his hair greased back. An oily, devious grin lit up his face. "Hey," he said. He beckoned Derek closer.

"Yeah?"

"I, uh, got what you need," the fairy hissed.

"Huh?" All he needed was a one-way ticket out of fairyland, and a guarantee he'd never, ever have to come back.

The fairy slapped Derek on the back. He tried not to shrink away. "More stuff. Magic. See, they want you to fail."

"What?" Derek said, suddenly interested. Maybe this guy knew something after all.

"Think about it," the fairy hissed. "You fail, they tack on more time. You don't want to play that game."

"Yeah." He most definitely did not. But . . . where did that leave him?

"Thousand bucks."

"What?" Derek yelped.

The fairy shushed him, shooting a look over his shoulder. "How bad do you want this to end?" he whispered.

Bad.

Really bad.

Derek sighed. "I'll give you a check."

CHAPTER 10

Derek didn't have long to wait before trying out his new equipment. He got another assignment the next night. He was almost glad — he couldn't wait to see the look on Lily's face when he didn't fail after all.

For once, he got there before Tracy and didn't bother to wait. Instead, Derek just pulled out his new bottle of invisibility spray and gave himself a quick shot. After giving the spray a few minutes to work, he headed for the front door. Before he could even try the knob, the door swung open.

A woman appeared in the doorway, humming an upbeat tune. But the moment she glanced up, she gasped.

Derek looked down at himself in alarm. He wasn't invisible after all — or at least, not *completely* invisible. He was transparent! Panicking, he plunged a hand into his tool pouch and grabbed something at random. It was the shrinking ste — not his first choice, but it would have to do. As the woman lurched backward, he squeezed the tube into his mouth and sucked down the paste as quickly as he could.

But the familiar shrinking sensation never came. Instead, it felt almost like his head was getting bigger. So wide that it would barely fit through the doorway.

"What's happening?" the woman shrieked. "What's going on with your head?"

"Just stay calm!" Derek shouted, squeezing his hands against his head to try to stop it from expanding. When that didn't work, he rummaged for his amnesia dust. He'd just wipe out her memory and start all over again. No harm, no foul. "You will now forget everything!" he commanded her, blowing the dust in her face.

She sneezed. A dazed expression came over her. "Oh, oh my," she said in wonderment. "I'm five years old in New York City, and my cat, Walter, is licking my face. I'm ten, and Billy Brenner is asking me for my lunch money but instead I dump my apple juice on his head, and now I'm in my dorm room, and — *that's* where I left my blue purse — what's happening to me? Wait a minute! I know you."

Derek groaned. This was getting worse by the second.

"You're Derek Thompson!" she squealed. "That washed-up hockey player also known as the Tooth Fairy who hails from Sioux Falls, Idaho, and has played for the Ice Wolves for the past eight point seven years! And now your head is back to normal. What's going on here? I'm calling the police!"

"Super-remembering dust," Derek muttered, slipping into the house while the woman groped for a phone. "Great." He searched frantically for a kid's bedroom. One door led to a giant utility closet. Another was a bedroom, but there was no one in it but a snoring old man. Derek ducked out quickly and headed for the third room on the hall.

Bulls-eye.

There was a six-year-old boy curled up in bed, sucking his thumb. Derek tiptoed into the room, stepped nimbly over a pile of discarded toys, and snatched the tooth from under the kid's pillow. He replaced it with a folded-up bill, and crept out of the room. The kid didn't even move.

When Derek got back to the front door, the terrified woman was long gone. He crept out of the house, unable to believe that things had gone so smoothly. Sure, there'd been a few wrinkles up front, but —

"COME OUT WITH YOUR HANDS UP!"

Floodlights lit up the front of the house. Sirens blared as a fleet of police cars roared into the driveway. Searchlights raked the street. Derek ran to the first hiding place he saw.

Unfortunately, it was a trash can.

He peeked over the edge. It seemed like the entire police force was lined up, aiming their guns in his direction. And he was pretty sure they weren't fooled by the trash can.

"*COME OUT WITH YOUR HANDS UP!*" a cop shouted again, through a megaphone. The command echoed in the night air. Derek racked his brain to come up with an idea. Something, anything, that would let him escape.

But he'd never been much of an idea guy.

He came out with his hands up.

"It wasn't my fault!" he shouted, walking toward the police slowly. The chaos of the night was starting to catch up with him, and he wobbled on his feet.

"Turn around and put your hands behind your back, please," the closest cop ordered him.

Derek did as he was told. He craned his neck toward the sky, searching in vain for a fairy vortex. "Fairies!" he cried. "Poof me up! Quick!"

The cop was looking at him like he was insane.

"Where's my magic wand?" Derek muttered, reaching for his tool kit. It was about then that he finally realized his tool kit was gone. So were his wings and his uniform. He looked just like a normal guy again. A normal guy who'd broken into some woman's house and was now muttering about magic wands and reaching into his coat pocket.

"He's got a gun!" the cop shouted.

It was only the five nearest cops who tackled him, but it felt like the whole force. Derek went down for the count.

Jail was a lot dirtier than it looked on TV.

Derek sat alone in the corner of the holding cell, trying his best not to make eye contact with the other prisoners. He counted the cracks in the cement wall, wondering how things had gone so wrong.

Without warning, his view of the wall was blocked by a fairy-shaped object: Tracy. Derek shook his head. So the fairy could blink into existence behind bars whenever he wanted, but he hadn't lifted a finger to get Derek *out*?

"You're amazing," Tracy said, leaning against the bars of the cell. "Lily's not happy about having to send in another fairy to clean up your mess."

Derek plunked his head into his hands. "I learned my lesson, okay?"

"Oh, and FYI, your sentence has been extended," Tracy informed him. "Lily just tacked on another week."

Derek groaned. "Just what I need."

But Tracy wasn't done. "Listen. I can get you fresh supplies, on a few conditions: From now on, you follow the rules, you embrace the fairy spirit, *and* . . . you listen to your caseworker."

As usual, Derek had no choice. "Fine," he said, giving up. "Deal. I will be the best tooth fairy ever."

There was a blinding flash of white. Derek squeezed his eyes shut against the glare, and when he opened them again, Tracy was gone. But Derek found a fresh pouch of magic supplies in his pocket. The good news was, Tracy had held up his end of the bargain.

The bad news: Derek was still in jail.

"Mr. Thompson?"

Derek opened his eyes, squinting against the light. His neck was killing him, along with his shoulders and his back. He must have slept funny — the bed felt hard as a metal slab.

It *was* a metal slab.

Derek sat up abruptly, realizing where he was. The night before hadn't been a nightmare after all.

"Mr. Thompson?" Louder this time, and significantly less polite. The voice belonged to a guard, standing in the door of the cell. It was open. "Your bail's been paid."

So Tracy came through after all, Derek thought, following the guard through the police station. But when he got into the public waiting area, the caseworker fairy was nowhere to be seen. There was only Carly — and she looked *mad.* Before he could thank her for posting bail, she turned her back on him and stormed toward the exit.

Derek grabbed her arm, trying to get her to stop and look at him. "It was a big misunderstanding," he pleaded. "Trust me, I'm still the same guy I always was —"

Carly whirled around, her face red and blotchy. "No, you're *not*. First, you keep running out on me to see I-don't-know-who. Then, you don't call, and when I finally *do* hear from you, it's to bail you out of jail? What's going *on* with you, Derek?"

"I want to tell you," Derek said, and in that moment he realized there was nothing in the world he wanted more. "But . . . I can't."

"Why not?" She stared at him, defying him to lie.

And because he didn't want to lie to her, but he wasn't allowed to tell the truth, he just kept his mouth shut.

"I know what this is," Carly said, a wrinkle creasing her forehead.

I seriously doubt that, Derek thought.

"This is you acting out because you're afraid of commitment," she said. "You're nervous about us getting serious, aren't you?"

Derek was about to deny it, when it occurred to him this might be the perfect solution. After all, what was more believable — that he was afraid of commitment, or that he was the tooth fairy? "Yes," he said, with as much sincerity as he could muster. "I'm nervous about us getting serious."

"What?" Carly cried, enraged.

Oops. Without thinking, Derek stuffed his hand in his pocket, reaching for his new tool pouch. Panicked, he tossed a pinch of amnesia dust into Carly's face.

"No," he said this time. "I'm not nervous about us getting serious. I never even *think* about getting serious with you!"

"What?" she shouted, even angrier than before.

If at first you don't succeed . . . Derek dosed her with another puff of amnesia dust and tried again. "Look, you're a woman. You wouldn't understand."

"*WHAT?*"

More panic. More dust. One more try. And this time, he inched just a little closer to the truth.

"I'm scared of messing it up and never finding another woman as perfect for me as you are," Derek said hopefully.

He held his breath, waiting for another explosion. But instead, Carly threw her arms around him. "Oh, Derek!" she squealed, burying her face in his chest. "It's okay. I'm just so glad you shared that with me."

Derek sighed in relief. Over her shoulder, one of the cops gave him a thumbs-up, then pointed to the pocket containing the amnesia dust. "Where can *I* get some of that?"

CHAPTER 11

Two whole days passed without any word from the fairies. But Derek didn't allow himself to believe it was over. Instead, he spent the time making plans. And when Tracy showed up with a new assignment, Derek was ready.

Well, almost ready.

"Come on, Derek!" Tracy shouted from the living room. "We gotta roll!"

"I'm coming, I'm coming." Derek was in the bedroom, putting the finishing touches on his project. He took his time, determined to get it right.

"Hurry up!"

"Hey, I've been stepped on, flushed, bitten, and arrested," Derek pointed out. Didn't he deserve some kind of break? Or at least a couple extra minutes?

"Dude, stop complaining!" Tracy called. "You promised to embrace the fairy spirit —"

"Oh, I'm embracing the fairy spirit all right," Derek said, finally showing himself.

Tracy's eyes widened in shock. Derek was wearing his usual fairy uniform. But he'd made a few . . . adjustments. He'd layered the uniform with his Ice Wolves shoulder pads, elbow pads, and jersey. Along with all the padding, he wore a helmet to cushion his head from any unexpected accidents (or dog attacks). The face mask would prevent anyone from recognizing him. As for the hockey stick . . . well, he didn't know whether that would be useful or not, but he always felt better when it was in his hands. If he had to play this tooth fairy game — and it looked like he did — he was going to play it *his* way.

Derek almost hoped that the kid would wake up. He wanted a chance to show off his new uniform. But the boy never stopped snoring.

It's for the best, he thought. *Maybe just this once, everything will go smoothly.*

Then the door eased open. A shadowy figure stepped into the room — and froze, when he saw a giant winged hockey player looming over his son.

"I'm just here for the tooth, sir," Derek said, in his deepest, most intimidating voice.

The kid's father opened his mouth. He drew in a deep breath, clearly readying himself to unleash a major league scream. Derek slapped a hand over his mouth before he could. "Shh, you'll wake him. Now, stay calm," he whispered, reaching under the pillow with his free hand. He wrapped his fingers around the tooth and slipped it into his pocket. "You're not going to remember any of this, okay?"

Trembling, the man nodded his head up and down so hard Derek feared he might nod it right off.

"Good," he said. He let go, and braced himself for a scream.

But the man just gaped at Derek. "Who are you?" he asked in a hushed voice.

Derek paused in front of the open window and struck a superhero pose, hands on hips, head held high. "I'm the tooth fairy." Then he dusted the man with amnesia powder and leapt out the window.

Just one problem: Derek still didn't know how to fly. He flapped his wings as hard as he could, just like he'd been told. But the ground kept getting closer and closer, way too fast. *Fly*, he urged his wings, waving his arms to create some kind of updraft.

The grass below the window was thick — but not thick enough.

"Aaaaaaah!" he screamed, landing with a painful thud, then tumbling head over heels. He rolled to a stop a couple inches from the sidewalk, where Tracy was waiting. Derek grinned up at the caseworker fairy, triumphant. Thanks to all the padding, nothing was even bruised (except maybe his ego). He pumped his fist in the air, then opened it to reveal: the tooth.

Mission accomplished.

Once he'd done a little attitude adjustment, Derek started to see an upside to the whole fairy thing. *Why not have a little fun with it?* he thought.

Which is how he ended up the next day at the edge of the ice rink, watching Mick Donnelly's pre-game interview with a smile on his face.

"So, how're you enjoying your time with Lansing?" asked the reporter.

Mick shrugged. "It's been all right. Nice being the new blood and all. Some of these Wolves are getting a little long in the tooth, if you know what I mean." He shot a glance at Derek, who greeted him with a perky thumbs-up.

"I assume you're talking about Derek Thompson, a.k.a. the Tooth Fairy?" The reporter's eyes gleamed with the promise of a juicy story. "Is that a little rivalry I'm sensing?"

"Rivalry?" Mick chuckled. "No way. I respect my elders. Dude's a legend. He started playing hockey in the Ice Age."

As Mick and the reporter laughed together, Derek reminded himself to stay calm. It was only a matter of time before Mick got exactly what was coming to him.

It was, in fact, a matter of eleven minutes. Derek had intended to wait until the second period of the game, but he ran out of patience.

"Mick, get ready!" the coach shouted. Donnelly jumped up and headed for the ice.

Derek got ready, too.

"Hey, good luck out there, buddy," he said to Mick cheerfully. "I mean it. I think you're going to do a *great* job, because you're the bestest hockey player *ever*. I wish I was you."

Mick looked at him like he was crazy. "You've gotten hit in the head one too many times, Thompson."

Derek just smiled. He waited until Mick was on the ice and the coach's attention was focused on his new star player. Then, while no one was watching, he snuck off the bench and rushed to the locker room. *Here goes nothing*, he thought, dousing himself with invisibility spray. Seconds later, he vanished.

Back on the ice, Mick skated to the center of the arena and took his position in the face off. All eyes were on him. No one noticed the gate to the players' area swing open by itself, as if by magic. As Mick raised his stick, no one could see the two invisible skates glide across the ice, and no one heard the low chuckle a few feet behind Mick, where there seemed to be nothing but an empty patch of ice.

The ref dropped the puck. The opposing center slapped it toward the Ice Wolves' side of the arena. Every player on the ice skated after the puck — every player except Mick. He tried, but something was gripping his jersey, holding him back. Mick scrabbled his feet on the ice, looking like a dog on a newly waxed floor, but he stayed in one place. He peered over his shoulder to see what was going on — at the exact moment that the invisible grip let go. He nearly fell on his face.

Mick regained his balance and sped toward the puck. He'd almost reached it when a mighty invisible force slammed into him, tossing him into the boards like a rag doll. The crowd booed, thinking he'd tripped over himself. What kind of a hotshot can't even stay on his skates?

"What's going on?" Mick muttered, chasing the puck again. He didn't get far before a very strange, prickly sensation swept over him, like someone was tickling him under his armpits and around the waist.

"Coochie coochie coo," bodiless voice cooed, sounding eerily familiar. Mick tried to stay in control, but the tickling got worse. He couldn't help himself — he started to giggle. Then he burst out laughing.

Soon he lost it completely, standing stock-still in the middle of the ice, his head thrown back in hysteria. His mouth was wide open, making it ridiculously easy to drop a certain fairy mint down his throat.

When the ref skated over to get some answers, all Mick could do was bark like a dog.

"Donnelly!" the coach roared, his face purple with rage. "Get off the ice."

Head hanging low, Mick skated back to the bench. With his head in his hands, he didn't notice Derek slipping in from the dressing area and sitting down next to him. "So, what'd I miss?" Derek said cheerfully, patting his invisibility spray with a silent *thank you*. "You do okay, buddy?"

Mick looked up at Derek, his face a portrait of misery. "*Woof.*"

Derek never got the chance to celebrate his victory. Just after the game ended, his cell phone buzzed with another tooth fairy appointment. *No big deal*, Derek thought. *After taking down Mick Donnelly, retrieving another tooth should be a piece of cake.*

He was right. The *retrieving* part went just fine. There were no bewildered fathers or angry dogs or hissing cats or shocked grandmothers. But there *was* a string of hockey-stick shaped letters on the wall, spelling out GABE'S ROOM. And lying in bed just beneath them, there was a familiar boy with bright red hair. It was the kid Derek had met outside the hockey arena, back when "Tooth Fairy" was just a nickname. The kid he'd told to give up hockey forever.

Judging from the crumpled hockey posters littering the floor, the kid had listened.

I don't feel guilty, Derek told himself. *Someone had to tell him the truth. Why not me?*

Still, he shoved an extra fistful of cash under Gabe's pillow. Maybe that would make up for it.

Maybe not.

Derek grabbed a notebook from Gabe's desk and scribbled out a message with the hockey stick–shaped ballpoint pen. He hesitated a moment, not sure this was a good idea. But it felt right. So he slipped the note under Gabe's pillow. When the kid woke up that morning, he'd find five dollars, and a suggestion:

Dear Gabe,
Please don't quit hockey. You're really good.
Love, the Tooth Fairy

*   *   *

After dropping the tooth off with Lily, Derek went in search of his caseworker. He found Tracy kicking back in the fairyland break room, flipping through an old issue of *Fairy Monthly*. "You sent me to Gabe's room on purpose, didn't you?" Derek accused him.

Tracy glanced up at him, feigning innocence. "What do you mean? He's on your route."

"Whatever. I made the exchange."

Tracy tossed the magazine on an empty chair. "But that's not all you did, is it?"

Derek looked away. "So I left him a few bucks extra. Is that not allowed?"

"I'm talking about the note," Tracy said, with a small smile.

Derek wasn't surprised that they were spying on him. He was too distracted to be angry. He kept remembering what he'd said to Gabe about giving up hockey, and the miserable look in the kid's eyes. "I don't know," Derek said, slumping into a chair next to Tracy. "He just looked so pathetic sleeping there, his little posters torn off the wall . . . I couldn't help myself." But even as he said it, he was starting to wonder if he'd done the right thing. "I put him back on that bad road again," he admitted. "'Disappointment and Heartbreak, two miles ahead.'"

"So why'd you do it?"

"I told you. I felt sorry for him."

"Yeah. Either that, or . . . somewhere in the back of your mind, you were thinking, 'Hey, what if he's that one in a zillion kid who's gonna be the next Gretzky?'"

"That's not what I was thinking," Derek snapped. This whole conversation had clearly been a mistake.

But Tracy wouldn't stop pushing it. "Or maybe, just maybe, he reminded you of, oh, I don't know, *yourself*? When you were a kid? And you still thought anything was possible?"

Derek stood up. It had been a pretty good day, and there was no way he was ending it on such a downer. "I'm done for the night," he said, heading for the door.

"You can't handle the tooth!" Tracy shouted after him, laughing.

Derek was determined to forget the whole thing. But that was easier said than done. And later that night, when he closed his eyes and tried to fall asleep, all he could see were those crumpled posters on Gabe's bedroom floor.

CHAPTER 12

Tooth fairying wasn't the only thing going better for Derek. Ever since that night at the police station, things with Carly were back on track. Even Randy seemed okay with having Derek around — especially once Derek promised to help him get ready for the school talent show.

Once Derek cleared out all the moldy boxes of old hockey magazines, his garage made a pretty good practice space. Randy came by every afternoon to rehearse on his guitar. Some days, Derek even pulled out his old drum set and played along. He wasn't very good, but who cared? There was no one to hear him but Randy, and Randy was too focused on his own mistakes to notice.

"I'm not gonna be ready," he complained, after messing

up for the third time in a row. "I'm gonna get up there and blow it."

"You'll do fine," Derek assured him. "You've just gotta keep practicing." But he could see the kid didn't believe it.

"Everyone's gonna laugh at me."

"Maybe," Derek said. Because it was true: Maybe they would. "Or maybe you'll blow the roof off the place." Because that was true, too. "You'll never know if you quit. You can't score if you don't take the shot."

"Yeah? When was the last time *you* took a shot?"

A surge of anger blasted through Derek, but it faded away just as quickly. The kid had a right to ask. "Listen. When I started out, I was a winger." He didn't like to talk about it; he didn't even like to *think* about it. "I was three-time All-American. First round draft pick of the Devils, playing in the NHL . . ."

"So what happened?"

Derek rubbed his shoulder. *Bad luck*, he thought. That's what had happened. No matter how talented you were, no matter how hard you worked, there was nothing you could do about bad luck. "Busted my shoulder one night in Chicago. So they sent me to the minors to recover. But it took forever. I got so angry and frustrated, I got into it with some meathead from New Haven, and knocked out a couple of the guy's teeth. The crowd went crazy." He smiled faintly at the memory. There he was, the lowest point of his career, feeling like an old puck, all scuffed and beat-up and ready for the trash — when the crowd had jumped to its feet and started to cheer.

"They called me the Tooth Fairy, and it stuck. Haven't scored in years." Derek took a deep breath. Saying it all out loud had been easier than he'd expected. And the story had a happy ending, right? "I have more penalty minutes than anyone else in the league!" he bragged, only half-joking.

Randy didn't even crack a smile. "But isn't your shoulder all healed now?"

"It's not the same as it used to be."

"But how do you know?" Randy asked. "You don't even try. You can't score if you don't take the shot."

Derek opened his mouth to say, *You don't know what you're talking about*. His shoulder might not hurt anymore, but it would never be the same. Nothing would ever be the same — it wasn't just the injury, it was *him*. Derek was the Tooth Fairy, the big guy who lurched around on his skates and knocked guys' heads together. The mascot; the joke. Nothing was going to change that.

Or was that just an excuse?

Randy drummed his fingers against the body of his guitar, waiting for an answer.

"Tell you what," Derek said, nodding toward the guitar. "I will, if you will."

Randy grinned. "Okay, I'll take that deal." He hoisted the guitar, ready to give the song another try.

Practicing hockey might not have been any harder than practicing the guitar, but it was a lot more painful. Derek hadn't realized how out of shape he was. Being the Tooth Fairy on the ice definitely didn't require much skill, which meant he had to get back to basics. Long, hard afternoons of drills, skating back and forth across the ice until his muscles screamed and he could barely stand. Weaving through a series of cones, over and over again until he could get the puck from one end of the ice to the other without knocking down any of the cones (or himself). Firing pucks into the net, one by one, never quitting until he got it right.

Every morning he was up at dawn for strength and endurance training — lifting weights in the gym, running miles through the neighborhood, doing pull-up after pull-up on the iron bar hung across his bathroom doorway. Every night he dropped into bed, too tired to move. When he closed his eyes, he saw hockey games in his head.

It was painful, exhausting work — but it felt good. So good that Derek didn't even mind those nights when his cell phone buzzed and the prickly feeling rippled across his shoulder blades. After all, collecting teeth was a lot easier on the arm muscles than doing another thousand pull-ups. Even Tracy had lightened up, although for some reason, he was always glum by the end of the night.

"Must be good, man," Tracy said one night, on their way out of Lily's office. They'd just dropped off another tooth. Derek wondered if he was racking up some kind of record. "That moment when you hand over the tooth. What does that *feel* like?"

Feels like handing over a tooth, Derek thought. *What else?*

But there was something about Tracy's expression, a mixture of hope and regret; there was a sad, wistful note in his voice. Derek finally got it. Tracy wasn't curious.

He was jealous.

Derek almost felt sorry for the guy. Sure, Tracy could be uptight and annoying — but he'd helped Derek out of more than a couple tight spots. Derek had gotten almost used to having him around. You might even say they were becoming . . . friends.

"Why don't you try and find out?" Derek encouraged him.

"What do you mean?" Tracy asked. "I don't have —"

"You don't have wings?" Derek finished for him, tired of the excuse. "So what? Show 'em you can compensate with other strengths. Speed, agility, flexibility."

"How am I going to do that?"

Derek just smiled. Tracy might know more than he did about being a tooth fairy. But when it came to getting in shape to take on the impossible, Derek was an expert.

"You want to be a tooth fairy, you've got to go for the tooth!" Derek shouted, as Tracy stumbled through a tooth fairy obstacle course. "Go! Go! Go!" he cried, blowing his whistle in Tracy's face.

He jogged alongside as Tracy struggled to climb over a tall fence. "You can do it!"

But Tracy couldn't, not on his first try.

And not on his second, or his third, or his fourth.

But finally, he was able to haul himself over the fence, landing in a triumphant heap on the other side. Derek gave him a few moments to feel proud, then tooted the whistle again, urging Tracy on to the next obstacle. The caseworker fairy faced a fake dog, a cardboard cutout that popped up and growled in a fake yard. He squeezed his way through a bedroom window — only slamming it down on his fingertips the first few times. He eventually made it through the fake living room with the fake wide-awake parents, shouting and calling the fake cops.

Every time Tracy got frustrated, every time he wanted to give up, Derek was there. In his face, cheering, shouting, blowing the whistle, urging him on. "You can do this," he assured the fairy, time and again. "I know you can."

And then one day, after hours of hard work, missteps, mistakes, and slammed fingertips, Tracy ran the whole course flawlessly. He scaled the wall in seconds. He squirted a stream of shrinking paste at the pop-up cardboard cut-out of a bulldog. He got through the window without breaking any glass, tossed amnesia dust on the pop-up parents, dosed himself with some invisibility spray just before the pop-up kid caught a glimpse. With a smooth, practiced motion he snatched the tooth, then climbed out the window and found himself dangling several feet from the ground.

A winged fairy could have just let go and floated away.

But Tracy didn't let his lack of wings stop him. He tied a rope to the window frame, giving it a sharp tug to make sure the knot would hold. Then he grabbed the rope and jumped, rappelling down the side of the fake house.

Derek had never been so proud.

The next time he saw Lily, Derek decided to put in a good word for his friend. "You know, you should give Tracy a shot at being a tooth fairy. He might surprise you. He's got potential."

Lily screwed up her face like she smelled something rotten. "Tracy's not a winged fairy."

"But why do you need wings to collect teeth? I mean, I've only got one that works. I don't even use mine."

Lily looked surprised. Derek wasn't sure whether it was because someone had dared talk back to her, or because she'd never thought of it like that before. And Derek wasn't going to give up. One way or another, Tracy was going to get a tooth.

A real one.

A few days before the talent show, Randy finished his guitar practice with a flourish — an impromptu solo riff that blew Derek away. "You're gonna kill out there!" Derek told him.

Randy grinned. "You think I could be a famous rock star?"

Uh-oh. Derek knew where this was going. He'd seen it way too many times before. Usually with bright-eyed junior hockey players, but it didn't matter whether you were talking about the NHL or the Rock and Roll Hall of Fame. The odds were still the same.

"Well, you want it straight?" Derek said, ready to launch into the same speech he'd given a million times.

Randy nodded.

"All right. You're getting pretty good, right?"

Randy ducked his head, but couldn't hide his proud smile.

"But let's say you keep working at it. Really hard. And before we know it, you're the best guitarist of all the thirteen-year-olds in your neighborhood. Here's the deal. You gotta remember, there are lots of other *neighborhoods*, and that means there are lots of other —" Derek hesitated. There was something familiar in Randy's face. Something familiar in the way he looked up at Derek, waiting to hear how he could fulfill his dreams.

It reminded Derek of another kid.

One who'd torn all the hockey posters off his walls. A kid who, thanks to Derek, had given up on his dream.

"You know what?" Derek said suddenly. "Yeah. It's possible."

And why not? Derek thought, rubbing the spot on his shoulder blades where he sometimes sprouted magic fairy wings. *Anything's possible, right?*

These days, no one knew that better than him.

It was late in the third period, with the Ice Wolves down four–three to the Plattsburgh Lumbermen. Derek sat on the bench next to Mick Donnelly, who'd been playing like an all-star. The coach had them on alert, ready to go in as soon as the Wolves got the puck back into Lumbermen territory. "Okay, old man," Donnelly teased.

Don't get angry, Derek warned himself. *Save it for the ice.* "I just might surprise you."

Donnelly raised his eyebrows. But before he could fire back another insult, the Wolves' goalie cleared a shot on the goal and slapped the puck down the ice. The Wolves took position, and the teams changed lines on the fly. Derek and Donnelly leapt off the bench, just as one of the Lumbermen offense made a play for the puck. Derek tore after him, and slammed him with a rough hip check, sending him skidding across the ice. An Ice Wolf winger snagged the puck, shooting a perfect pass down the ice to Derek. Donnelly positioned himself in the Lumberman zone, readying for his shot.

But Derek faked the pass. His defender bought it, heading for Donnelly. The goaltender went for it, too, leaving Derek with a clear path to the net.

Donnelly smacked his stick against the ice, impatient for his pass.

Derek held on to the puck.

"Pass!" Donnelly shouted.

"Pass!" the coach shouted.

"Pass!" the crowd roared.

Shoot, Derek thought, raising his stick. He stared at the puck, at the undefended goal, and tried not to think about how this moment could be the turning point, how the whole game rested on his shoulders, how he couldn't afford to make a single mistake —

And then a Lumberman defenseman barreled into him. Derek flew backward and slammed into the boards. The Lumbermen took possession of the puck. Donnelly, without Derek to guard him, didn't have a prayer — he made it about a foot before the Lumbermen took him out and laid him flat.

Derek hadn't even stumbled to his feet when a miserable howl tore through the stands. The Lumbermen had scored. And all because Derek had hesitated a moment too long. Or because he'd been foolish enough to believe he could score in the first place.

"What were you thinking, Thompson?" the coach snarled as Derek took his place back on the sidelines. "You're a sideshow attraction, not a hockey player! You know what? You can watch tomorrow night from the bench!"

Derek didn't argue. How could he, after what had just happened? The coach was right: Thinking he could be a real hockey player again? What a joke.

The bench was exactly where he belonged.

*   *   *

By the time he got home, Derek was in the worst mood of his life.

Carly and the kids were waiting for him, big smiles smeared across their faces. Apparently they hadn't seen the game. "Derek, guess what?" Tess squealed. "I have another loose tooth!"

Derek couldn't muster much enthusiasm, even the fake kind. "Good for you, sweetheart."

"What's wrong?" Carly asked, concerned.

Talking about it was the only thing that could make his mood even *worse*. So Derek just shrugged. "Everything. Nothing. Forget it." He noticed that Randy had his guitar with him, and realized they were due for a rehearsal. "Hey, buddy, do you mind if we skip this session? I just don't have it in me."

"But the talent show's tomorrow night!" Randy protested. "I need at least one more run-through —"

"No, you don't." Derek sighed. Why wouldn't they all just leave him alone? "You'll be fine."

"No, I won't. We gotta keep practicing —"

"Dude, honestly, it doesn't matter!" Derek exploded. "Because chances are, no matter how good you are in this talent show, you're just another kid with a guitar. You're not gonna be a famous rock star, okay? You're not gonna be the lead guitarist standing *behind* the famous rock star. Do yourself a favor and just give it up!"

"Derek!" Carly cried.

"I'm sorry," Derek said. "But this is for his own good. Trust me." He'd made a mistake the other night, telling the kid a bunch of lies just to make him feel better. Like he'd been telling himself lies all this time.

It *didn't* feel better.

Randy's eyes watered. For a second, Derek thought he might burst into tears. But instead, he hoisted his guitar over his head and smashed it violently to the ground. With an echoing clang, it snapped in two. Now the tears began to fall. Randy grabbed his little sister's hand and dragged her toward the car. He shoved her in first, then got in beside her. Shooting Derek a betrayed look, he slammed the door behind them.

"What's wrong with you?" Carly shouted at Derek, her face white.

"I had a really bad day, okay?" Derek said, realizing he might have gone a step too far.

"A bad day?" Carly repeated, incredulous. "You had *a bad day*?"

"Yeah, I —"

"No, Derek, it's *not* okay," she said slowly. "You're never going to talk to my kids again. We're done." She stormed to the car.

"Wait!" he cried, terrified that he was about to lose the last thing that mattered.

Carly ignored him.

So he followed her, stopping her before she could get into the car. Carly wouldn't even look at him. "You know what your problem is, Derek?" she said, in a low, cold voice. "You don't ask 'What if?' and you never will."

He didn't argue. He just stood in the driveway and watched as she got into the car and sped away.

Derek went straight to bed. The next morning, he didn't get up at dawn to work out. He didn't get up at all until the afternoon, when the doorbell rang. And even then, he only bothered to answer it on the off chance it might be Carly.

It wasn't.

It was Tracy. He was practically glowing. Derek resisted the urge to slam the door in his disgustingly cheerful face. "What do you want?"

"Guess what happened today?" Tracy exclaimed.

"You won a gold medal in the Olympics?" Derek guessed sourly. "You got picked to sing the fairy national anthem in the fairy World Series?" He yawned. "I'm going back to bed."

"Lily gave me *this*!" Tracy flipped open his wallet to reveal a shiny tooth fairy learner's permit. "She said, 'You've got potential.'" He was bouncing with excitement. "But the important thing is I'm on the road."

"Good for you," Derek said flatly. "Don't let the door hit you on the way out."

"This is all because of *you*. You're my man."

"Yeah, well, this man needs another five hours shut-eye, so good-bye —" He tried to shut the door, but Tracy shoved his foot in and wedged it open.

"Aw, come on," Tracy said. "We gotta celebrate —"

"*Celebrate?*" That was the final straw. He'd tried being polite, but Tracy just couldn't take a hint. So Derek would spell it out for him. "I just lost everything that matters to me. My girl, those kids . . . I think I just hung up my skates for good. All because I bought into this fairy stuff. And look where it got me."

"What? You make one effort after all these years, and when it doesn't work out, you just give up?" Tracy shook his head. "It's not supposed to be that easy. And you know it."

Who did this guy think he was, calling him a quitter? "I'll tell you what I know," Derek snapped. "You can keep trying to be a tooth fairy all you want. You don't have wings.

What happens if you have to escape from a ten-story building? I'll tell you what happens." He smacked his palm against the doorframe. "*Splat.*"

Tracy didn't even flinch. "You know what's really sad? The one you've hurt most with all your dream-killing isn't Randy or Carly or even me. It's you."

"Get out!" Derek shouted. Tracy could spout all the fairy wisdom he wanted — but he'd be doing it on the other side of the door. Before Derek could slam the door in his face, he disappeared.

Derek was alone. But Tracy's words still lingered in the air.

Was he right? Derek wondered.

Even if he was, what did it matter? Derek had messed everything up. He'd ruined his career, he'd driven away Carly and the kids. There was nothing left he could do.

There's always a way, said a voice in his head. Except it wasn't Tracy's voice this time.

It was his own.

CHAPTER 13

The next day, the Ice Wolves played their arch-rivals, the Fort Wayne Roughnecks. Derek had been tempted to just skip the game. After all, there was little chance the coach would let him play — now, or ever again. So what was the point in suiting up?

But he did it anyway. Put on the familiar uniform, laced up his skates, and joined his team on the sidelines. Whatever else had happened, he was still a member of the Ice Wolves. Right now, that was pretty much all he had left.

Even if he'd be watching the game from the bench.

The game was a disaster. The Ice Wolves racked up penalty after penalty, as the defensemen tried to fill the hole Derek had left behind. His replacement, Andreas Petrenko, did the best he could, but the Roughnecks surged ahead.

Mick Donnelly was playing with bruised ribs, which meant that he wasn't getting much time with the puck. Still, he was playing his heart out. There were two NHL scouts sitting in the front row.

Mick took a shot at the net, but the puck slammed into the crossbar. As the Wolves scrambled to regain possession, Petrenko got a brutal hip check from the Roughneck offense and went down. Moments passed, and he didn't get up. A whistle blew, stopping the action. The crowd fell silent as the team doctors skated onto the ice and hovered over him. Finally, they helped him to his feet and guided him over to the side. The crowd cheered — but even though Petrenko was still in one piece, he was out of the game for good. The Wolves were now down one defenseman.

Derek could do the math — and so could his coach.

The coach turned to Derek, looking disgusted. He sighed, then flicked a hand toward the ice. "Thompson. Go."

For a moment, Derek was too surprised to move. He'd expected never to play hockey again, and now —

"*Go!*" the coach roared.

Derek went.

He should have been thrilled to get back on the ice. But once he was there, head down, stick in hand, he realized he didn't want to be there at all. Not if he had to play the Tooth Fairy, the team joke. What was the point?

His team was counting on him, so he did his job. He went through the motions. But when the Roughnecks got possession of the puck and drove it into Ice Wolves territory, he didn't really care.

One of the Roughnecks caught him off guard and hammered him into the boards. Derek's head slammed into the smashproof glass. The helmet cushioned the blow, but a loud ringing echoed through his ears. As the other players chased the puck down the ice, Derek shook his head, trying to clear it. The buzzing noise faded, but it was replaced by something else. Voices.

Memories.

I want to play in the NHL, just like you used to. . . .

You hung up your skates a long time ago, Derek. . . .

You don't say 'What if?' and you never will.

Suddenly, movement above the Roughnecks' goal caught his eye. He blinked, hard, but the figure was still there, sitting atop the goal. It was Tracy.

The caseworker fairy nodded at Derek, and suddenly, he knew what he had to do.

A Roughneck wingman had possession of the puck. Derek launched himself toward the player. The guy cringed, expecting a jaw-crushing blow from the Tooth Fairy.

But Derek didn't smash into the guy or knock out his teeth. Instead, he slashed his stick with lightning speed and stole possession of the puck. The Roughneck defensemen surrounded him, but Derek had been practicing his stick-work for weeks. He moved around them with ease, faking left, faking right, slicing the puck through their legs and around their clumsy feet. One of the Roughnecks slammed his stick into Derek's face. But Derek shrugged off the blow and charged toward the goal. Soon there was nothing but a clear patch of ice between him and the net. He had a shot — now all he needed was the nerve to take it.

"No!" the coach shouted, when he realized that Derek was setting up.

Derek ignored him. This time he wasn't going to over-think things. He wasn't going to let the moment slip by. He raised his stick — just as a Roughneck defenseman charged him, knocking him off his feet. Flying through the air, Derek managed to swing the stick forward. It made contact with a sharp crack, and the puck sailed down the ice, past the goalie . . . and straight into the goal.

"Thompson shoots and scores!" The announcer's voice boomed through the arena. The crowd rose to its feet, whooping and cheering. Derek couldn't believe he'd taken the shot — and that it had actually gone in. He'd waited a long, long time to have this kind of moment again. He wanted it to last forever.

It lasted approximately five more seconds, until he spotted Tracy on the sidelines, pointing to his watch. Derek knew what that meant.

"No," he murmured. There was a brief break in the action as the players took their positions, and Derek skated over to Tracy. "I can't leave now," he insisted under his breath. He was pretty sure he was the only one who could see the caseworker fairy, and he didn't want to look insane. Especially not *now*. "This is my last chance to actually *play* the game, to go out the way I came in."

Tracy understood. "I can cover for you. After what I just saw, you deserve it."

The game was starting up again.

"Thompson, what are you doing?" the coach shouted.

Derek had to get back out there. But this was important, too. "You're just a trainee. Isn't that breaking the rules?"

Tracy had never met a rule he wasn't desperate to follow. But apparently that was the *old* Tracy. "I learned from the best. But I do think you should look at the address before you decide."

Derek glanced at the scoreboard, which was flashing an address. Carly's address.

A whistle blew. "Thompson!" the coach shouted. "You get back out there, or you're finished."

Derek froze. The coach wasn't kidding. If Derek left in the middle of the game, it was over for him. No one would ever hire him again.

"I can go," Tracy offered. "Lily doesn't have to know."

"Yeah. But *I'll* know." Derek looked from the coach to Tracy, to the address on the scoreboard, and back to the coach again. For his whole life, all he'd ever wanted to do was play hockey.

But maybe that was the *old* Derek. Maybe things had changed.

"This is my house to take care of," he said.

Tracy smiled proudly. And then his face went pale.

Derek was about to ask why — when he felt the prickling in his shoulder blades. He was spouting fairy wings . . . in front of an entire audience of hockey fans!

The game ground to a halt. Everyone on the ice and off turned to gape at Derek in his sparkling fairy uniform.

"I knew you had it in you," Tracy said, pulling a pouch of amnesia dust from his pocket. "Don't worry. I'll take care of them. Go."

It was going to take more than a couple handfuls of amnesia dust to deal with this. A *lot* more. But if Tracy said he could handle it, Derek was willing to trust him. Besides, he had somewhere to be.

He skated to the back of the rink, then circled the goal, trying to build up some speed. He made another circuit, flapping his wings until they caught air, and he lifted off the ground. He soared through the arena, higher and higher, as the ceiling burst into a sparkling cloud of white light. Derek sailed straight into the heart of the dazzling glow, and disappeared.

Derek rematerialized in Tess's bedroom. She was sleeping on her side, arms hugged tight around a teddy bear. With a practiced gesture, Derek slipped the tooth from beneath her pillow and replaced it with a dollar bill. Then he leaned toward her left ear. "Psssst."

Tess stirred, but didn't wake up.

"Tess," he whispered, a little louder.

She opened her eyes, then bolted upright. "Derek!"

He shushed her. Carly was down the hall, asleep on the living room couch, and he didn't want to wake her. "Hi, honey," he said softly.

Tess giggled at the sight of his sparkling wings. "Hi, Derek. I like your costume."

Derek smiled, and sat down on the edge of the bed. "Listen. I gotta tell you something. I was wrong. The tooth fairy is real. And it's *me*."

She giggled again, like he'd pointed out the most obvious fact in the world. "I know."

He tried to make her understand. "No, I'm not talking about the hockey Tooth Fairy. I'm talking about the *real* tooth fairy."

She rolled her eyes and gave him a Randy-like look. "No, you're not."

Oh, really? Derek waved his hands over her head, and a shower of fairy dust floated over her, surrounding her in a sparkling, rainbow-colored halo of light.

Tess's eyes got very big. "You *are* the tooth fairy!"

Derek brought a finger to his lips. "It's a secret, okay?"

"Okay." She nodded, her eyes shining. "Wow!"

Derek stood up, wishing he could stay. He had a feeling his next task wouldn't be quite so easy. But it had to be done. Waving good-bye to Tess, he tiptoed down the hall and slipped into Randy's room. Randy was lying on the top bunk, his back toward the door. He had headphones on, and didn't hear Derek come in. That gave Derek the chance to grab a blanket from the lower bunk and wrap it around his wings. Randy wasn't like Tess; he was too old to believe in tooth fairies. He needed a different truth.

Derek reached up and nudged Randy's shoulder. Randy turned over and pulled off his headphones. He scowled at Derek. "What are you doing here?"

"I need to talk to you."

Randy turned away again. "Go away."

Derek sighed. But he wasn't going anywhere. If he had to talk to Randy's back, then that's what he would do. "Randy, those things I said yesterday . . . I was wrong."

There was a pause. "I don't care."

"You've gotta keep playing guitar, Randy. Because you're good. And because nothing you love doing that much could ever be a waste of time. I'm so sorry."

"Yeah, well, I can't play anymore even if I wanted to," Randy said, his voice muffled, like he was talking into his pillow. Or trying not to cry. "I smashed my guitar, remember? And tonight was my talent show."

Derek felt even worse. He'd forgotten about the talent show. And now there was nothing he could do.

Or was there?

He pulled out his magic wand and rested his finger on the All-Purpose Magic Generator Button. The one that had never worked before. He closed his eyes.

It does whatever you want it to, the fairy had promised. *But you have to believe, or it doesn't work.*

Derek believed in Randy. He believed in fairy magic.

And, for the first time in a *very* long time, he believed in himself.

So he pressed the button.

He opened his eyes, hopeful. For a moment, nothing happened. Then a sparkling puff of fairy dust shot out of the wand. When the cloud dissipated, there was a brand-new guitar sitting on the lower bunk. He'd done it! Derek held the guitar up for Randy. "Here. Maybe this will help."

Randy sat up, gaping at the instrument. "Whoa! It's awesome . . . how did you do that?"

"All-Purpose Magic Generator," Derek said quickly. "Now put some clothes on! We can still make the talent show."

Randy jumped off the bunk bed. He hesitated for a moment, totally confused. Then he threw his arms around Derek. The hug was great — except that it knocked off the blanket covering Derek's wings.

Randy stepped back in shock. "What are you *wearing*?"

There was no time for fake explanations. (Even if Derek had one. Which he didn't.) "Just get dressed!" Derek urged him. "You'll see in a minute. Hurry!"

Everything was working out perfectly.

Well, almost perfectly.

"*Derek!*" Carly's angry voice rang through the house.

Derek could have jumped out the window and flown away. After all, he had the tooth. But he trudged into the living room to face Carly. Before he could say anything, Tess hurtled into the room, still in her pajamas. "Mommy, Derek is the tooth fairy!" she shrieked.

Carly looked him up and down. "You rented a fairy costume to make it up to Tess?" she said.

"Yeah, sure." It was as good an explanation as any.

"Mom, Derek got me a new guitar!" Randy ran into the room waving his new instrument over his head.

Carly looked bewildered. "You got him a —?"

"And he's taking me to the talent show!" Randy added.

"Derek, I don't even know . . ." She trailed off. "Wow. This is . . . amazing." She folded him into a hug.

Derek felt an enormous weight slip off his shoulders. "Hey. Anytime." He said it casually, like it was no big deal. But it was the biggest deal in the world.

Carly pulled back. "But there's no way you'll get to the talent show in time. It's gotta be almost —"

"Yes, I can!" Derek exclaimed. *Nothing* was going to get in the way of his happy ending. "You and Tess get dressed and meet us there, okay?"

She looked skeptical.

"Just go!" Derek urged her.

Carly gave in to the chaos. She grabbed Tess and swept her away to get dressed. As soon as they were gone, Derek pushed Randy out the door.

"Where's your car?" Randy asked, looking around for the blue Camaro.

"No car. Let's go."

"What?"

Derek didn't answer. He was too busy flapping. He wrapped his arms around Randy, hoping he'd be strong enough to hold both of them in the air. He took a running start, flapping his wings even harder, and leapt into the air. They were flying! Randy's jaw dropped open. He grabbed hold of Derek's arm and squeezed tightly.

"How is this possible?" Randy asked as the ground dropped out beneath them. Soon they were hundreds of feet up in the air. Derek looked out at the landscape spread out beneath them, miniature houses and lawns stretching to the horizon. The people were the size of ants, and the cars looked like toys. "See, it all started when I got this ticket under my pillow . . ."

Derek told Randy everything, from start to finish. He finished just as they reached the school. That's when it occurred to him that he had never learned how to land. He crossed his fingers, hoping it would just come naturally. He began flapping a little slower. It seemed to work — they dropped toward the ground, gently at first.

Then they fell faster.

Too fast.

"Ow!" Randy grunted as they tumbled to the ground.

Derek climbed to his feet, then gave Randy a hand. "Gimme a break. I haven't really worked out my landings yet."

They had landed just outside the school's auditorium. Faint notes wafted into the night. The talent show had already begun. Randy would have to hurry if he was going to make it inside. But first —

"Sorry, buddy," Derek said, reaching into his pouch, "but I've already broken enough rules." He tossed the amnesia dust into Randy's face.

Randy looked dazed. Before he could say anything, a teacher popped his head out the stage door. "Randy! We've been looking all over for you. Get in there and tune up!"

Randy turned to Derek, confused as to how he'd ended up at school, with a brand-new guitar in his hands. Derek pushed him through the door before he could ask any questions. As the door swung closed again, Derek leaned against the wall, heaving a sigh of relief.

He'd actually done it.

A familiar breeze blew past, whipping into a frenzy. A sparkling cyclone whirred into existence, opening the vortex to fairyland. This time, Derek took a flying leap into the center of the whirlwind and closed his eyes against the flash of blinding white.

CHAPTER 14

Derek found himself in Lily's office, as usual. He tossed her the tooth. There was no time to waste. "Listen, I got a show to catch, so —"

"You skirted quite a few rules tonight, Mr. Thompson."

"What?" Derek exploded. She *still* wasn't satisfied? "I covered with Carly, I dusted Randy. And Tess — so what? She's only six! Pretty soon, she'll forget. Or not. And what's the harm? This way, she'll always —" He broke off.

"Always what?" Lily encouraged him.

Derek knew what she was getting at. And he wasn't about to give her the satisfaction. "You know."

Lily turned to Tracy, who stood obediently by her side. "What was that, two tons of amnesia dust you had to use in the arena?" She raised an eyebrow at Derek. "I should bill you *and* tack on another week —"

"Always believe!" Derek exclaimed, defeated. "Okay? I was wrong! I get it! Kids need fantasies because they teach them how to dream. And dreams are good. For all of us. All right? Can I go now?"

Lily smiled warmly. "Congratulations, Mr. Thompson. You are hereby relieved of fairy duty."

At her words, his wings vanished.

"Wow," Derek said, impressed. "You're good."

She held out a hand for him to shake. He laughed. "Put that thing away." He pulled her into a bear hug.

Lily broke away from the hug and pulled something from her jacket pocket. "Tracy, step forward."

"Wait, what's this?" Tracy asked nervously.

"Anyone who can rehabilitate Mr. Thompson more than deserves these," Lily said, opening her hand to reveal a pair of delicate silver wings. There was a silver tooth perched in between them. She pinned the wings to Tracy's lapel.

"Oh, this is wonderful!" Tracy gushed, a blush spreading across his face. "They're beautiful. Thank you."

Tracy deserved his moment of glory, but Derek couldn't help glancing at his watch. "Okay, this is all very nice, but I've got a concert to get to."

Tracy and Lily exchanged a solemn glance.

Uh-oh, Derek thought. *What now?*

"Tracy, would you do the honors?" Lily said.

Tracy lowered his head sadly.

"What?" Derek asked, getting seriously worried. "What are you talking about? What's he gonna do?"

Lily handed Tracy a small pouch. Tracy dumped a pile of dust onto his palm. "Sorry, buddy. You won't remember any of this. At least, not the magic part."

"Why not?" Derek asked, surprised to realize he was sad. He didn't *want* to forget what it had felt like to be the tooth fairy. He didn't want to forget his new friends.

"Because that's just the way we do it," Lily said.

"I'll never forget you, man," Tracy promised him.

Derek had never been very good at the whole emotion thing. But Tracy had become a good friend. "I can't believe you showed up at the rink," he said awkwardly, hoping Tracy would understand how much it meant to him.

Tracy smiled modestly. "It's what we do."

"Thank you. Take care of yourself . . . you four-eyed giraffe." They both laughed faintly at the insult, remembering the days when they'd been at each other's throats.

Then Tracy embraced him. "You're my man," he said.

Derek clapped him on the back. "You're my fairy." He stepped back, vowing never to forget his friend.

Then Tracy tossed a handful of dust in his face.

And fairyland faded away.

*　　*　　*

Derek found himself in the auditorium of Randy's middle school. He had no idea how he'd gotten there. Carly flagged him down. "There you are! I couldn't find you!"

"Yeah, I —" Derek paused. *Where was I?* he thought, confused. He searched his memory, but it was blank. "I couldn't find you, either," he said finally. Whatever had happened, he had Carly back again. That's all that mattered.

They found seats in the crowded auditorium, just as a teacher announced the next performer: Randy Harris.

Randy took center stage. He hoisted his guitar and, looking nervously out at the audience, strummed the first note. As he played through the song, his anxious expression faded. And the more confident he got, the better he played.

"He's really feeling it!" Derek whispered.

Derek realized he'd never been happier. Sitting in this auditorium with Carly and Tess beside him and Randy shining up on stage, he had everything he'd ever wanted. It wasn't just about Carly, it was about all of them. It was about being a family. And he didn't want it to end.

He took a deep breath and leaned toward Carly, his lips brushing her ear. "Listen, I was wondering," he whispered. "What if we got married?"

Carly whirled to look at him, speechless.

"Did you hear me?" Derek asked. "I said, '*What if?*'"

CHAPTER 15

The wedding was originally planned for the beginning of October, but they had to postpone it. After all, it's tough to get married on the same day you're playing in the season opener of the NHL.

Derek's first game with the LA Kings was a success. The team won three to nothing — thanks to Derek's two goals at the end of the third period. He skated off the ice in a daze. Getting engaged to Carly, getting the call from the NHL . . . overnight, his life had turned into a fairy tale.

Almost like magic, Derek thought as he changed into his street clothes. Of course, there was no such thing as magic.

Everyone knew that.

Still, he couldn't help feeling like something, or someone, was looking out for him. And if they were, he owed them.

A crowd of fans was waiting for him as he came out of the locker room, all of them clamoring for his attention.

"Mr. Thompson!"

"Can I have your autograph?"

Derek loved every minute of it. One little kid with scruffy brown hair pushed his way to the front of the crowd and stuck a program in Derek's hands.

"There you go," Derek said, scrawling his name across the page. "What's your name?"

"Oliver," the boy said, gazing up at Derek. "When I grow up, I'm gonna play hockey in the Olympics!"

"Good for you, Oliver." Derek smiled. "Go for it."

And he meant it.

As Derek signed program after program, he looked up to see a familiar man standing before him, a curious smile on his face. "Can I have one, too?" the man asked, extending a program.

Derek searched the man's face for some clue to his identity. He was about Derek's age, with sandy brown hair, glasses, and an anxious manner. Derek couldn't shake the feeling that they knew each other. "What's your name?"

"Tracy," the man said, looking at Derek expectantly.

"Tracy," Derek tested the name, trying to remember when he would have said it before. "Isn't that a girl's name?"

Tracy laughed and shook his head.

Derek signed his name. "There you go, Tracy."

"Thanks." The man turned to leave.

"Hey, wait." There was just *something* about this guy. "You look familiar. Do I know you?"

Tracy smiled, but there was a hint of sadness in it. "I don't think so."

Derek shrugged, and let the guy walk away. Must be he just had one of those familiar faces. Besides, Carly and the kids were waiting. They threw their arms around Derek, gushing about how amazing he'd been on the ice.

But he couldn't help watching Tracy as he disappeared into the crowd. "I swear I know that guy," he mumbled. Carly didn't hear. She was too busy chattering about how proud she was that Derek had achieved his dreams.

Soon Derek embraced his new family, the strangely familiar man forgotten. He didn't need to sign autographs. He didn't need fame and fortune and a Stanley Cup. All he needed were a pair of skates, a hockey stick — and a family.

As long as they were together, they could do anything. Maybe there was no such thing as magic; maybe there were no fairy-tale happy endings. But that didn't mean you couldn't have dreams. Derek understood that now.

Because sometimes, against all reason, against all odds, dreams come true.